Always Close the Gate Behind You

Russell Harlow Ingalls

Galina,

I just wanted to say thanks for letting me help you with your home purchase. I am also very happy that we have a young teacher moved to our area to educate our kids. Please let me know if you need anything. Always,

Russ

ISBN: 1451581475

ISBN-13: 9781451581478

After the sudden, accidental and near simultaneous deaths of both his parents and grandfather, Dana Thompson, days after celebrating his first birthday, inherited his grandfather's nine hundred acre farm.

The year, 1939, was a time in this northeast corner of Vermont when grown men struggled to feed their families, hold onto their farms and still nurture their dignity as the clutches of the great depression held strong. The lifelong battle against the elements alone made just carving out a living a daily ordeal.

Follow Dana Thompson's life as he is rescued by strangers unknown and raised, while his benefactors try to keep the local banker and land baron, Robert Marcoux, from stealing this prized land, an untouched virgin maple forest, a land of unimaginable proportion and riches. Marcoux's interest is no more than to log, rape and pillage this jewel buried deep in the north woods of this ancient land with no regard of history, heritage and tradition. When Dana's grandfather's account is depleted, Marcoux is eager to lend young Dana and his caretakers' money needed to keep the farm from the hands of the tax collectors, knowing all the while it is he, Marcoux, who at a time of his choosing will be the ultimate beneficiary.

Watch this incredible story of Dana's life unfold as he comes of age, discovers his real family and how his role in life is both extraordinary and nearly unimaginable. Witness his battle to save his grandfather's farm from the clutches of evil, his only connection to his past. See the simple and ingenuous acts of kindness proving once again the greatness of these people who will sacrifice everything but their honor and loyalty to live in this curious land they call the northeast kingdom.

Preface

This book started on a deer hunting excursion one fall November day in northern Vermont, 1998. As I walked from our camp I came across an old stone wall that ran straight and true, disappearing through the trees up over the hill that I was about to climb. Knowing that stone walls were usually boundary markers made when farmers stacked rocks on their property lines when they cleared their fields, I envisioned how hard they must have worked to clear this forest that must have been grown up as much then, as it was now.

Soon I stumbled upon the old field stone foundations of the house and the large granite pieces that marked where the barn stood the two hundred or so years before.

I am not a stranger to the woods of Vermont nor was this the first time I had ever seen old foundations that far back in thc woods when I was sure that I was the only white man who had ever stepped where I was standing. But this time something was profoundly different.

As I explored the area around the two old foundations, I found an apple orchard of a dozen trees or more that was a short distance away from both, that were arranged in such a way that convinced me that these early settlers were the ones who had planted them. As I stood in the middle of the orchard and looked back towards the cellar holes and then further to the stone wall that originally caught my attention, I started to get images of people who might have been responsible for cutting my hunting trip short.

I found myself back to the stone wall where I followed it curiously to see where it would lead me. I got to a corner where the wall turned to the right, and saw a big, old maple tree growing up through the stones marking the boundary line as well. On every corner thereafter was a huge maple tree.

I followed the wall until it returned me to where I first discovered it two hours earlier. At that instance, I realized this book was written inside my head completely how you are about to read it except for a few chapters that begged to be written as I was translating it to paper.

I have many people to thank for inspiring me that I wish to acknowledge here and many more that I will thank personally, face to face.

Thanks to Charles "Chuck" Powell and Donna Underwood, may you both rest in peace. Thanks to Garrett Keiser as well. They were my English teachers in high school that passionately taught and pushed their students to explore their inner selves and to let us believe that writing was as simple as sitting down and putting it on paper.

My good friend, Guy, encouraged me to write. 'If for only five minutes, write every day,' he tells me. Guy is more disciplined than I.

Trisha Needham is the person who tirelessly edited what I wrote and took a lot of rough thoughts and words and put polish to them, allowing me to just write, no matter how bad it was.

Deborah McCormick read every word and chapter as I wrote it and acted as if it was the Pulitzer Award, giving me the encouragement and inspiration to continue on that every author needs when you feel you've hit a wall. I found also, that books take a long time to write and without her support of many ways, this book would have still been in my head and not published. She is the girlfriend that is so much more.

Owen "Gene" Plants and James "Buddy" Loux, who sadly passed away before I finished the book, are two people who I want this book to be dedicated to. They are my friends who I think about and miss every day. Both lived their lives to the fullest and with no regrets.

Gene, may the mountains of West Virginia forever echo your rebel yell.

Buddy, May your dives be deep and your mountains tall, may you rest in eternal piece, you've inspired us all.

I hope you enjoy my book.

Russ

Chapter 1

Sitting in the court house in attorney Fred Summers' office, Dana Thompson was thinking how alone he felt even though he was accompanied by his aunt and uncle. The reason the three were sitting there was the result of a tragic story Dana was part of but never controlled.

Dana, at the age of one year old, as the only surviving heir, inherited from his grandfather, Joseph Lanou, a nine hundred acre farm. Now at the age of fifteen he was there to sign it over to the local land baron, Robert Marcoux, in lieu of money owed.

It was an early spring day in northern Vermont. The sun hadn't shown all day.

The sky was jam-packed with thick, dark, angry-looking clouds, threatening to unload their fury at any time.

The snow still on the ground was dirty and unkempt, not beautiful, new and smooth, like it was in December when it looked like a Christmas blanket spread beneath the Christmas tree.

It was a few minutes before four in the afternoon. The lumber mill would be letting out soon. A slow line of tired people would trudge up the hill to the town to collect their mail and grab a few groceries that were needed for supper.

Most of them would, in short time, make their way back down the hill to the Mill village where they lived and where some in town would say, belonged. The town would then be quiet as the last bit of daylight would give way to darkness as though in a hurry to start the next day searching for sun.

Joseph Lanou had lost his wife to cancer. They had one child together, a daughter. She was twelve when her mother died and life without her mother's guidance was hard for her. It was difficult for Joseph too, but that was an emotion that he wasn't able to express. To do so would have admitted weakness.

His daughter and he fought bitterly and continually. There was no happiness between them, only contempt, and on her part, hatred. It was only when she was nearly seventeen years old did she find happiness again.

He was a boy from the school she met, when he occasionally attended, who she felt understood her. He listened to her when she spoke. He was born and raised in the Mill village. His family came the first day the mill opened and surely would be there the day it closed. She was the most beautiful thing that had ever paid him any attention. It was love at first sight.

It was only a short time before Dana was conceived and the two soul mates eloped. It was the mother's wish the baby not be born out of wedlock.

Dana Thompson arrived in this world August 14th, 1938.

It wasn't that Joe Lanou wasn't proud of his new grandson, or that he didn't love his daughter. It was that Dana's grandfather and father, it was told, hated one another. His grandfather wanted better for his daughter and grandson and certainly, he was convinced, they wouldn't find it in this third generation 'mill rat'; Dana's father only wanted better for his young family.

Between his new father- in- law's constant meddling, and the continuous barrage of mean- spirited comments that were leveled at him for marrying somebody from town instead of someone from the village, delivered by his work mates with whom he worked side by side and lived, Dana's father had heard enough. There was a better life for them elsewhere.

Elsewhere was seventy miles to the south. He had been hired to work in the granite quarries in Barre, Vermont. He would finally leave behind the mill and the village that had consumed his old family for years. His new family would be safe. In the fall of 1939 the borrowed car was loaded with a few busted-up suit cases, none full, ready to make the journey south.

After stopping at a few places to say their goodbyes, one of them being Joe Lanou's where the two men could sling their final insults at one another, the new family of three pointed the car towards the new world. It was a beautiful fall day. The sun was bright and sometimes blinding without a cloud to hide behind as it hung low in the late afternoon sky.

Onward south they travelled with the front windows slightly down an inch or two so that the cool air flowed into the car filled with the smell of the last hay crops of the year along with the fields of corn that were beginning to be harvested. The trees that lined the roads and filled the mountainsides were displaying their vibrant colors of orange, red and yellow leaves which, when contrasted against the brilliant blue sky, seemed more spectacular than ever. Most were still attached to their limbs, waiting for the winds and rain of fall to blow them to the ground and be scattered in every direction. "How could anything that is dying be so beautiful?" Dana's mother asked his father.

Down the old country road that followed the river through those healthy fields of hay and corn, occasionally catching the honking voices of the Canadian geese that formed huge V's in the sky seemingly urging the geese and the car further south, they all traveled. Past farms and through towns that had survived for generations living off the land and depending on one another.

The car continued along the twisty road as the sun pounded through the windshield, sometimes making it difficult to see. It was here, forty miles south of Ethenburg, with the baby asleep on the floor in the back, where Dana's father stretched over to the passenger side to kiss his wife, that the car then drifted left of center, into the path of that big truck, ironically carrying a huge slab of granite stone for cargo.

It wasn't a fair collision, or pretty. The car lay mangled across the road, its front occupants thrown partially through the windshield where their lifeless bodies came to rest on the hood of their borrowed car. The truck sat where the impact occurred, moderately damaged, with the driver unscathed, at least physically.

News traveled slowly in 1939 on a late Saturday afternoon in rural Vermont.

It started with the news of a terrible accident. The local people on scene knew none of the 'out of towners' who lay dead in the car. Only when the outpost State trooper arrived did the scene begin to take order. After determining that there were no survivors, he interviewed the driver of the truck and anyone else who might have witnessed the accident.

When the medical examiner had given permission to remove the bodies, the process to identify the occupants began. The plates and registration revealed who the vehicle belonged to. They did not match the identification found on the deceased. The trooper searched the personal belongings of the occupants, finding enough evidence that the deceased were in fact who he believed they were.

The trooper completed his report. Only then did the news start its journey north, following the same twisty country road. Slowly, like the evening fog forming on the river, it travelled, blanketing everyone it touched with sorrow and unanswered questions.

A few hours later in the fading daylight, a sheriff's car drove up the gravel drive leading to Joe Lanou's homestead. Curt Briar, the newly elected Sheriff was behind the wheel. *No lights on in the house but I had better check there first,* he decided.

Officer Briar walked up the few steps and knocked loudly on the heavy door. He turned to wait for someone to answer, practicing in his mind what he'd say. No words came; this was the first time he'd ever had to notify the next of kin.

He knocked again, this time turning toward the barn as he waited, scanning for any signs of life.

Sheriff Briar stepped down off the porch when the knock went unanswered and headed toward the milk house. Long eerie shadows leapt across the drive when he walked in front of his cruiser headlights. The sheriff reached for his coat collar to protect his cheek from the cool north wind breeze that had picked up. A nearly full moon had started to crest the silhouetted western mountain ridge line. *Looks like we could get a frost tonight,* the sheriff thought, as he reached for the handle to the milk house. The door opened before his hand made contact.

A tired-looking man in overalls and a dirty cap greeted him with no smiles or words. An uncomfortable silence settled between the two. The sheriff was the first to speak.

"Are you Joseph Lanou?" Officer Briar asked.

"Yes, I am," the farmer answered, "What has that no good son of a bitch got my daughter into now?" he angrily asked.

The officer stared at the man, shaken by his response, collected himself and spoke. "I'm sorry to be the one to tell you sir, but there has been a terrible car accident. There were no survivors."

The Officer readied himself for another verbal assault but none was forthcoming. He watched the farmer's stiff body start to slump, his head slowly dropping until he was looking at the ground between them. After what felt like an eternity to the sheriff, Joe Lanou took a deep breath and slowly let it out, his eyes still looking at the spot of earth between them. He raised his head slowly and looked at the officer, his face, which a few seconds before had been taut, was now drained and defeated. "Thank you for coming by," he said softly, and shut the milk house door.

Officer Briar stood staring at the door momentarily. He felt relieved, but was sad for the farmer. He hoped he had said the right words. It was all that came to mind. He thought it was odd that the farmer hadn't asked any details.

I'll give him a couple hours then I'll swing back in to see if he needs anything and answer any questions.

The Officer walked back to his cruiser. He pointed the car down the gravel drive and drove into town, stopping at the gas pumps at Johnson's store. *I might as well fill the cruiser for Monday,* he thought. As he stood there waiting with the nozzle in the filler tube, Charlie Johnson, the store's owner, came out onto the broad, brightly-lit porch, and leaned over the railing to get closer to the officer.

"I don't envy you," he said quietly.

"No Charlie, it wasn't a lot of fun. Thank God I don't have to do it very often," the officer responded, trying to sound as if he had owned his job for years when in fact it had only been a short while.

"It's just terrible," Charlie said. "And to lose that little baby boy too," he added sadly.

Officer Briar stood processing what the store keeper had just said. His head snapped towards Charlie with his eyes wide when it sunk in.

"What did you say?" he asked Charlie with an alarmed, puzzled look on his face.

Charlie stood up abruptly from the railing, thinking he had said something to offend the Sheriff.

"Well, ahhhh, you know, it's bad enough to lose the two parents and all but to have that little kid die, well, that's just terrible," Charlie said, choosing his words carefully, wanting to show his genuine concern.

The Sheriff stepped away from the cruiser and closer to the porch looking up at Charlie, their faces only inches apart.

"Charlie," the sheriff said almost under his breath, "there were only two people in the car."

"Curt," the store owner started, mirroring the sheriff's tone, "I don't know that. All I can tell you is, when those kids filled their car with gas here earlier today, they came into my store to pay and to say goodbye. They were going to live in Barre is what they told to anyone who would listen, and they had that baby with them."

Sheriff Briar looked at Charlie as if he had been kicked in the stomach, his mouth held open in disbelief. He ran to the steps and leapt onto the porch, making his way to the double doors of the store.

"Charlie," he yelled, "I need to use your phone."

Charlie led the sheriff to the back office where the phone was. They shut the door, as people gathered in the aisle outside the office wondering what the commotion was about.

Ten minutes later the door tore open. "I've got to go tell Joe!" the sheriff said as he ran down the aisle toward the front door.

Just before he reached it, one of the town men burst through the doors yelling, "Fire! Fire! Fire at the Lanou farm!"

"Shit!" the sheriff hollered as he burst out on to the porch and cleared the steps with a leap. He yanked the gas hose out of his tank on the way by and dove into the car. The cruiser roared to life. The officer slammed the car in gear. Smoke poured from the tires as the car whipped a u-turn in front of the store, heading south for the Lanou farm. The siren screamed to life to join the chorus of tires and racing engine with the red flashing emergency lights casting an eerie glow against the yellow painted store until the cruiser disappeared from sight.

The sheriff reached the drive a couple miles out of town in just a short minute, but it seemed like an eternity. The cruiser tore up the Lanou driveway spewing gravel as it fishtailed from side to side, searching for traction. An ominous orange, reddish glow lit up the evening sky as he approached the homestead in high gear. The sheriff saw seconds later what caused it. The house, the barn, and all the outbuildings were fully engulfed. The flames were leaping hundreds of feet into the twilight sky. A man's figure was silhouetted against the intense fire. *I hope that's Joe,* the sheriff prayed.

He slammed the car in park before the car had stopped moving, sliding to a stop. "Joe!" the sheriff hollered, exiting the car. The man turned. It wasn't Joe.

"I'm his neighbor," the man said. "Joe's nowhere to be found," turning back helplessly to watch the blaze as if he was mesmerized by it.

It would have seemed comical had it not been so tragic.

Everybody down south was talking about the two dead 'out of towners.'

The people up north had heard that there were no survivors; that two people had died.

The people up north were asking about the baby. "Where's the baby? Who has the baby? There was a baby boy in the car with his parents!" they cried.

The Trooper's report said there were only two people. Calls were made and the Trooper was dispatched again to search the car; he couldn't find it. The Trooper pulled up in front of the wrecker driver's house.

"I'm sorry to bother you at this hour," he said to the driver, "but there has been a report of a missing baby boy. They seem to think he was in the car."

“Ahh,” the driver responded, “they’re crazy. There ain’t nobody in that car.”

“I know,” the Trooper said, “but I need to do as I’m instructed. Can you tell me where it is?”

“Ah yup,” the driver responded, “I’ll do better than that, I’ll show ya. Let me get my feet dressed.”

The wrecker driver returned a few minutes later, hollering over his shoulder, “I’ll be right back, dear. Somebody’s taken some stupid pills.”

“I weren’t talking about you,” he was quick to say to the Trooper.

“I didn’t think you were,” the Trooper responded, “but I agree with you.”

“I parked it out behind the barn,” the driver said, “I don’t need a bunch of nosey town folk poking around. You can pull your car right around back,” he offered, swinging his arm around the right end of the barn. "Just follow the road."

The wrecker driver cut through the barn and was fishing for a flashlight from his truck when the Trooper came around the corner, easily seeing the car still attached to the tow truck because of the near full, harvest moon. He directed his headlights on the mangled wreck.

The Trooper exited his vehicle and was shining his flashlight inside the front of the car when the driver joined him.

“Boy,” said the driver, “what a mess,” as he shone the beam over the shattered glass covered with dried blood and death, peering through his frosty breath.

“Sure is,” the Trooper answered.

The front windshield which the two front occupants had smashed through and both windows of the front doors were shattered. The rear doors were wedged shut but somehow the glass hadn't broken.

The two men were on opposite sides, shining their lights into the back seat.

Through their breath that distorted their flashlights' beam, they both noticed the rear bottom seat cushion had flipped up and wedged itself against the front seats from the force of the crash.

Both tried the rear doors on their sides. They wouldn't budge.

"You got a pry bar?" the Trooper asked.

"Ah yup," the driver responded. "Let me get it out of the truck."

The wrecker driver returned a few moments later with a four foot bar and joined the trooper on the driver's side of the wreck.

"Pry right here," the Trooper said, pointing with his flashlight before laying it on the ground behind him, "and I'll work the handle and pull."

Working together, the pair managed to create a six inch gap. The driver used his bar for leverage and with the Trooper pulling, they managed to increase the gap by better than a foot.

"Wait a second," the driver said, "Let me squeeze my body in there and then I can use my feet to push against the car."

The smaller man did just that. The metal groaned and creaked in protest as it was forced from its jammed position. The door was now fully open.

"Let's get this seat flipped up and then we can go home," the Trooper directed. The two positioned themselves in the narrow entrance.

They worked on the jammed seat bottom cushion together and were able to squeeze their fingers into a gap to get the cushion to wiggle. The wrecker driver grabbed his bar.

"Be careful with that just in case," the Trooper cautioned.

"I will," the driver assured him.

He worked the bar in the gap as he had done with the door. The wedged cushion popped up, flipping back to its intended position. The dark floor was now exposed.

"There," the Trooper said, "let me get my light," as he quickly reached on the ground behind him.

He directed the beam on the floor of the rear driver side and then to the passenger side when he saw some movement. It was then they found what the people up north had said all along was in the car.

A baby! An alive baby boy, wrapped in his blanket!

It was at that moment that the terrified baby began to cry, along with the Trooper and wrecker driver.

Chapter 2

As slowly as the news had traveled earlier in the day, the news of the miracle baby sped north as fast and furious as a summer lightning storm.

The trooper and the wrecker driver rushed the baby into the house where they called the local doctor. While they waited for him to arrive, the wrecker driver's wife tended to the terrified baby. When she was able to calm him down, she fed him and then lovingly bathed him in the kitchen sink.

The Trooper called his superiors and was ordered to bring the baby home to his kin after the doctor gave his o.k.

Neither the trooper nor his superiors would have known that they had issued an order that was impossible to complete. Baby Dana's parents had died in the crash. His grandfather had determined his own fate. There was no one left.

The doctor arrived, and after giving Dana a complete and thorough examination announced that he hadn't so much as suffered a scratch. He was fit to be reunited with his family!

The Trooper asked the wrecker driver and his wife if they would ride the forty miles to bring the baby home.

"I don't think we could pry that baby from her arms," the wrecker driver said with a rueful smile.

The trooper went and readied his car for passengers while the wrecker driver and his wife prepared themselves and the baby for the trip.

The wife sat in the back holding the baby while the two men took the front seats.

The Trooper flipped on his siren and lights and proceeded north.

"Do you think it's possible, sir, that you could shut the siren off and just use your lights? The noise is scaring the baby," the wrecker driver's wife asked, adding, "he acts like he would like to go to sleep."

"Ma'am, I do not have a problem with that," the trooper said. He turned the siren off.

"Thank you," she responded.

The Trooper drove to the end of the street and turned right. Driving through the center of town they passed the volunteer fire department.

Somehow, as it always seems to happen in a small town, the news of the miracle baby and his trip home had become known.

Waiting on the side of the road were a couple fire trucks with their emergency lights flashing. They pulled out and followed with their sirens on after the cruiser passed.

"Ma'am," the trooper said, "I won't be able to do much about that."

"I understand," she replied softly, "he's sleeping now anyways."

And so it went. Every small town they passed through people were standing on the sides of the road waving or honking their horns as the procession followed.

Every town added a couple vehicles to the end of the line. Some were fire trucks, there were a couple Sheriffs cars, and people followed in their own vehicles.

By the time the Trooper's car reached the Ethenburg line, there had to be twenty assorted vehicles making up the unlikely parade.

The procession of vehicles entered the village with the State Police cruiser leading. He drove slowly past the common and then turned right to circle back around to the Protestant Church. He had noticed a flashing red light of a sheriffs vehicle at the church on the far side of the common when he passed, obviously signaling them. The parade of vehicles that followed either blended in with the already assembled vehicles or headed back home, their duty done.

The Trooper shut off his lights and got out of the car. He paused by his door to observe the crowd. Most everyone's attention was focused in his direction. *I wonder who the next of kin is?* he thought, as he peered into some of the curious faces that were now not focused on him but the occupants of his cruiser. They peered into the night trying to get a glimpse of the baby, but respectfully kept their distance.

The sheriff, Curt Briar, was the first to approach him. They identified themselves to one another as they shook hands.

"How's the baby doing?" the sheriff asked the trooper.

"Surprisingly, for all that happened in his little world today, pretty damned good," the trooper responded, adding, "I'm here, as you know, to deliver him to his family."

"Well, Sir," Officer Briar said, drawing a deep breath and slowly letting it out, "that's where it gets messy."

"I guess I don't understand, Sheriff," the trooper said. "Just introduce me to them and I'll hand the baby over and be on my way, as long as they are able bodied people."

"Well," the Sheriff started again, "I don't mean to sound like a broken record but that's where it gets confusing. According to the town folk, all the relatives this kid had in the world died today."

"You've got to be kidding me," the Trooper said in disbelief. The trooper stood there shaking his head thinking, *things are just going from bad to worse for this little guy.*

"Wished I was but I'm not," the Sheriff said.

"So what do we do now?" the trooper asked.

"Well, you have a couple options," Sheriff Briar explained. "You can leave the baby with me....."

"No, no, no!" the trooper interrupted. "My superiors ordered me to turn this baby over to his family and you have no idea how much I screwed up today. This baby stays with me until I'm satisfied he's safe."

"Ok, then," Sheriff Briar said, "your second option is to join these people in the Town Hall for a meeting that they're having to determine who will care for this baby until Monday, when we can get some state guidance. They were just waiting for you before they started."

"Ok," the Trooper said. "Tell me what I need to do."

"Let me introduce you to some people, then we'll make our way over to the Hall," the sheriff said.

Sheriff Briar introduced the trooper to the Protestant minister, James Barberra, and then to Madeleine Dean, the Chair of the ladies' auxiliary. He looked briefly for the village moderator, David Williams, until someone told him he had made his way to the Town Hall lest somebody beat him to the podium.

"Ok then," the sheriff directed after he was sure that all the decision makers had been introduced, "let's get this show on the road."

The trooper walked backed to his car. He scanned the growing crowd again that now must have numbered a couple hundred. He looked at his watch before he entered his cruiser. It was eleven o'clock almost on the dot. *It's going to be a late night,* he thought, *but I think I owe this little boy more than that.*

Madeleine Dean expertly herded everyone towards the Town Hall a few buildings down. Madeleine made herself part of every important decision decided in town. Being the Chairperson of the Church's ladies auxiliary seemed to give her broad powers. It was joked around town that there were three things one should avoid in life. The first was peeing into the wind. The second was pulling on Superman's cape, Americas newly invented superhero. The third and most serious was, never get on the bad side of the Church's ladies' auxiliary!

The trooper entered the cruiser and explained what the plan was.

"You know," the wrecker driver's wife said after listening to what the trooper said, "we could keep him." She looked at her husband for support.

Catching his cue the husband said, "We'd be more than happy to."

"Yes, I can tell." the Trooper replied, "Unfortunately this is the avenue we are asked to follow for now, but I will make sure when the meeting starts to tell everyone what you folks have offered," the trooper promised.

"One thing I did tell the Sheriff though is that this baby stays in my company until I'm satisfied. If these people can't come up with a reasonable solution then I'm going to take you folks up on your offer for at least the weekend," the appreciative trooper said to assure the folks that the baby would be safe one way or the other.

He pulled the cruiser up to the Town Hall and waited until most of the gathered crowd had made their way inside.

The town folk flooded into the Hall searching for empty seats. No one was surprised to see David Williams already standing behind the podium ready to preside as he had done at every important event held in the village for the last thirty years.

The trooper opened the rear door and escorted his passengers up the stairs to the second storey where the meeting was to be held. The noisy crowd quieted when the wrecker driver and his wife entered carrying the baby. It seemed everybody was straining to view the miracle child, which was hard because of the protective way the child was insulated by the wrecker driver's wife from the chill of the fall evening air that seemed to follow the crowd into the Hall.

When everyone was seated, Moderator Williams dropped the gavel with precision. It sounded like a rifle shot had gone off in the cool building that nobody had thought to build a fire in. He loudly called the meeting to order. Madeleine, seated close behind, gave him hell as quietly as she could but was still heard by everyone present, pointing to the sleeping baby.

"Sorry," he mouthed towards the wrecker driver's wife, cringing after receiving Madeleine's scolding. She nodded that she accepted his apology.

"Could I ask the Reverend to lead us in a quiet prayer before we begin?" Williams asked, looking back at Madeleine as he finished his request.

The Reverend said some words of prayer asking the Lord for proper guidance and to bless those who had lost their lives today.

Moderator Williams asked the three newcomers to stand and identify themselves, which the trooper, the wrecker driver and his wife did.

The trooper, as promised, stood before the town folk and explained that his superiors had asked him to deliver this baby to his kin folk. He further explained that he realized the family had all passed and if the town folk could not agree who should keep the baby, or if they did decide and he wasn't comfortable with the decision, he would ask the folks who held the baby now to do so until the State could help on Monday to place the child somewhere safe.

That got the hall buzzing like a stirred-up beehive. Moderator Williams held the gavel high as a threat for those who were unruly to quiet down. Madeleine gave a few Shhhh's and the crowd quieted.

Moderator Williams decided that those who had an idea of who should care for baby Dana, for at least the weekend, should raise their hands and he would call on them so that they could voice their plea. He cautioned that those who couldn't be civil would be asked to leave.

The discussions began and after a half hour of resolving nothing the trooper was fidgeting. Many people had spoken but the only thing that was agreed on was to disagree. In only a few more minutes, he decided, he was going to make the decision that only his passengers wanted. It was a decision he didn't want to make but it would be a safe one, not only for the child but for himself as well.

Halfway through the middle of an argument between two townspeople, a soft voice interrupted, timid but determined, from the back of the Hall.

"Excuse me, excuse me," said the voice softly. The two people who were arguing stopped in mid- sentence. Chairs scraped on the hardwood floor as people turned to see who had interrupted the debate.

Standing there was Polly McCay, and a few steps behind her, clearly not enjoying the newfound attention, her husband David.

"Yes, how can we help you?" Moderator Williams asked.

Polly hesitantly walked a few steps closer and spoke. "I'm here to take my nephew home."

There was a loud gasp from the audience followed by incoherent, louder whispers.

"Quiet!" the moderator demanded when the gavel held high above his head did no good as people's attention had turned to the back of the Hall.

"Can you say what you just said again?" the moderator asked in disbelief.

Polly stood a little straighter and braver and said, "My brother died today with his wife, and I am here to take my nephew home."

The crowd was now almost ready to riot. The Trooper looked at Sheriff Briar and they both walked to the front of the Hall to quiet the crowd.

For some reason, and certainly not by accident, the fact that Polly was indeed this child's aunt had been overlooked. Maybe because the people in town never imagined that this child would go to Mill village, or maybe because Polly and David were so timid that some would have thought they were "foolish", a country slang for mental retardation. Whatever the reason, now that they had been reminded, most everybody in the Hall knew the relationship, though they didn't want to admit it.

When the Law Officers and Madeleine finally got the crowd under control, Polly, with David now at her side, spoke again.

"I'm sorry that so many of you had to come out at this late hour but I know many of you here know our relationship to this child. We just want to take our nephew home and then you people can go home as well," Polly said, speaking clearly and sternly, casting her gaze across the crowd. She cleared her throat and continued, "David and I are not rich people but we certainly make enough money to care for this child. He is our flesh and blood and we intend to take him home tonight," she said defiantly.

The trooper had listened closely when the woman talked. She spoke no worse than the others who voiced their concerns earlier;

in fact, she made more sense. Furthermore, if she was an aunt to the child then by turning the child over to her he could satisfy the orders of his superiors. He surveyed the crowd. Many of them had turned back towards the front of the Hall and had their heads down. *Just what have I got myself into?'* he wondered. *These people have known all along that this lady is this child's aunt.*

The trooper whispered something to the Sheriff. The Sheriff nodded and whispered something back. Both law Officers approached Moderator Williams. The three were quickly joined by Madeleine. The town folk strained to hear what was being discussed. The trooper seemed to be doing most of the talking. It was clear that whatever the discussion was about, Madeleine wasn't happy about it. The meeting broke up after just a few short minutes.

The trooper and the sheriff both walked towards Polly and David McCay. They led the couple to the back of the Hall.

"Good!" a man's voice said anonymously from the crowd. "Tell them to go back where they came from." A few more quiet affirmations seconded the out of order motion.

The trooper was asking the McCays some questions and Polly was answering. When they were finished all four smiled. The two law officers walked back to the podium and conferred with Mr. Williams and Madeleine for just a moment. They turned and faced the crowd as Moderator Williams smacked the gavel down three times, oblivious to the sleeping child. Duty called.

He addressed the crowd with all the pomp and circumstance thirty such years had earned him. "My fellow citizens, we have made a decision. The Honorable Trooper was instructed by his superiors of the Vermont State Police to bring this child to his next of kin. Can anybody stand before us and prove that Polly McCay is not the aunt of this child?"

Some loud and unflattering murmurs were directed towards the back of the Hall.

"Anybody?" bellowed the Moderator.

"By the Powers vested in me, I hereby instruct the Honorable Trooper to escort baby Dana to the home of Polly and David McCay."

With that the gavel came crashing down, adjourning the meeting. There was still plenty of grumbling, but the Moderator's decision was final.

CHAPTER 3

Life in Mill village probably wouldn't be called great for those who knew the difference. But for most it was all they knew or would ever know.

The Black River narrowed at that point, and two hundred years earlier its mighty falls had been harnessed, creating the largest mill in the area. Surrounded by woods teeming with every species of tree from the mighty oak to the lowly poplar, the mill seemed designed by God's own hand.

The Black river was joined by Lords creek a mile or two below Ethenburg where the rivers flowed north to the thirty-two mile long Lake Memphremagog, straddling the American and Canadian border. It was unusual for two such large river systems to be so close together, with the Black on the east of Ethenburg and the Lords on the west, and that's what gave the village its importance and history.

With both rivers headed north it was easy to get the logs to Canada and on to the St. Lawrence Seaway if that's where the intended destination was. The same could be said for anything that wanted to come south, like booze during prohibition or rationed supplies during all the wars America was part of, from the revolution, the civil war, both World Wars, or other conflicts.

It was in the Mill village that the people who created the legends and lore of the area were born and lived. It was in the Mill village where life was created for those who lived there because without the river, there was no life. But what made the Mill village most unusual was its name. The village was really just a collection of houses within the boundaries of the town of Ethenburg. It wasn't recognized on any map. It had no stores, post office or schools. No separate highway department, law enforcement or town government, but make no mistake, it had a life of its own.

People took care of their own problems, and when it spilled out into the streets, only then was the law called, with someone usually getting hauled off to jail for the night, locked up in Ethenburg until they could come before the judge or they sobered up, depending on the severity of what had happened the night before.

It was also understood that, for the most part, people from the village and town didn't mix. The mill people climbed the hill to do their business and then went home. And the people who lived on the hill in town stayed in town, unless they were into things they shouldn't have been. That's the way both sides preferred it.

It certain circumstances the two cultures collided, such as in the marriage and death of Dana's parents, although it didn't have to have such a tragic ending. Usually it was a battle that was determined by money and lawyers. Whoever had the most, won. Mill village usually was on the losing end because of the lack of both important ingredients. When Dana's parents died, both sides claimed him. This time those ingredients weren't the deciding factor. Blood is thick, family thicker. The Mill village had reclaimed one of their own.... and stuck it to the townspeople as well. Dana was a rare victory for the village. A victory over what was right and wrong. Both sides would have claimed that.

His aunt and uncle did what they were supposed to. They raised the boy the best way they knew. There was the visit from the State from time to time, checking on his well-being and also for the settling of his grandfather's nine hundred acre estate, but once the State awarded full custody to Dana's aunt and uncle, even those visits stopped and life in the village moved on.

Along with the inheritance of the land came some money that was left in Joe Lanou's account. Not a lot, but enough to pay the taxes for about seven years or so. There was the occasional offer to buy the property but David and Polly McCay were not business people. Besides, it wasn't their land to sell. The land belonged to Dana.

Dana and his adopted family got along without many problems. His aunt and uncle were good people, simple people. Dana understood from an early age that giving them problems would only create bigger problems for himself.

His uncle worked six days a week in the mill, and on Sunday was prone to abuse the bottle some. His aunt worked in a small business doing laundry for others, mostly for the town folks, and the hand-me-downs that were unclaimed or given came in handy to keep a growing boy clothed. She worked five days a week and half a day on Saturday which gave her time to keep the family affairs together. She wasn't a drinker; she had seen enough harm because of it. So Sundays were good days to spend with her nephew.

Out of all the things Dana loved to do, visiting his grandfather's homestead was his favorite.

On Sundays, when the weather was good, he and his aunt would walk the couple miles, each taking turns carrying the small picnic basket they had prepared. Walking up the old rough driveway, which certainly could have used some fresh gravel in spots, to the burned-out cellar holes where both the house and barn had once stood, gave Dana a real feeling of belonging. It was his identity. Even at an early age he could sense his family there with him. It was strange because there were no memories, only a sense of calm.

He would play among the old foundations, imagining what had once been, while his aunt laid out the table cloth on the old picnic table under the big maple, the table being the only thing that survived the fire. Together they would eat their sandwiches and drink the sweetened ice tea out of the same bottle, while Polly told stories about his father, her brother, and some of what she knew about his grandfather, grandmother, and mother, though she knew very little about them.

Even though he had heard the stories a thousand times before, he acted as it was the first time he had heard them. Sometimes he'd ask the same questions he'd asked the week before or if he could think of new ones, he'd ask those. Most times Aunt Polly couldn't answer the new ones, but that was okay because Dana would just imagine the answers.

After a couple of hours, which always went by way too fast, they would pack up their basket and head for home. One Sunday, as they were preparing to walk home, they could hear a vehicle approaching up the rough drive. They could hear the car's powerful engine racing at times, but it was the loud scraping of the car's underneath that got their attention. Whoever it was seemed oblivious to the large pot holes that were punishing the car.

After some curious moments the car finally came in to view.

It was and long and shiny and the whitest car Dana had ever seen. The sun gleamed off the polished chrome so much that it hurt his eyes when it reflected the sun's rays just at the right angle.

The car came to a stop. The cloud of dust that was chasing behind caught up, enveloping the car, making it momentarily invisible. The dust took a moment to settle. When it had, Polly and Dana realized a man had gotten out and was standing by the driver's door.

He was a short, pudgy man with a cowboy hat, dressed in an ill-fitting white suit that seemed a little tight in places, especially where his belly was.

"Hello," he spoke, "you must be Polly McCay," looking first at Dana's aunt.

"Yes, I am," she acknowledged. Dana sensed that his aunt was as uncomfortable as he had ever seen her.

"And you young man must be Joe Lanou's grandson," the pudgy man assumed correctly. Dana looked up at his aunt, not knowing how to respond or if he should, as not many times in his life had he been identified that way.

Dana's aunt spoke for him. "This is my nephew, Dana Thompson. His grandfather was Joe Lanou."

"That's what I thought," said the man. "Let me introduce myself," after he realized that Polly wasn't going to ask his name.

"I'm Robert Marcoux. I buy and sell real estate. I've inquired several times about this farm but I've also been told more than once that it isn't for sale. Is that correct?" he asked.

Polly felt very intimidated talking to this stranger. There was something about him that made her feel very uneasy. Even when he wasn't trying to talk down to her, he did. But it was something deeper than that.

"The farm is not for sale," Polly said flatly, really just wanting this man to go away.

"Great, then I won't bother you anymore. I hope you enjoy your day," the stranger said to the both of them.

He started to climb back into his car, but stopped and stood again.

"Excuse me for bothering you again, but I also am a director of the Bank of Ethenburg. It was brought to my attention the other day that you may not have enough money in your account to pay the taxes on this land this year. I would hate to see you lose this piece of property to a tax sale," he said with a smile that looked more like a smirk.

"Little Jr. here," as he motioned towards Dana, "is the rightful heir and we need to do everything we can to make sure this land stays in his family. If you run into any problems, please, just call me and I can help."

The stranger then came around and handed a card to Polly. She couldn't help but step back as he approached her, despite herself.

"My number is on the card. Don't hesitate to call. Or if you don't have a telephone, and I assume you don't, you can leave a message at the bank and I'll come see you," he offered, thinking he was being polite, but not making any extra effort if he wasn't.

The man walked to his car and slammed the door. He turned it towards the drive and scraped his way to the main road, again not caring if he hit the pot holes. Polly was glad he was gone. She didn't like him. There was something sinister about him. She packed up what remained of lunch, and she and Dana started their walk home.

Dana thought Aunt Polly was unusually quiet on the walk into town.

Polly couldn't shake the encounter from her mind. It bothered her. It seemed so strange as they walked into town along the common. Looking over at the white Protestant church, its majestic steeple reaching for heaven, it dawned on her what was bothering her.

Polly had always thought the devil wore red.

CHAPTER 4

Just as Robert Marcoux had warned, the money left in Joe Lanou's account had come to an end. After seven years the money that had paid the taxes on the farm was exhausted.

When Polly received the notice from the Town Clerk that nearly one thousand dollars were due for taxes, she and David did the only thing they knew they could do. To come up with that much money on what they made was not a possibility.

The phone call was made.

Marcoux was more than happy to pay the taxes, and continued to for the next six years. The deal with the devil had been made. There would be, they understood, a day that he reared his ugly head.

"Don't worry," he would always say. When Jr. was old enough something could be worked out. So on went the years, along with the debt, with interest too.

The day came on a beautiful fall Sunday morning. The brilliant blue sky was filled with big, puffy, pure white clouds. The air was crisp with no humidity. The freshly fallen multi-colored leaves scurried along the ground in the slight breeze as if they still had life.

The shiny, big white car pulled into the Mill village. It stopped out front of the uncluttered, tired- looking house that Dana and the McCays called home.

It was very unusual to see Mr. Marcoux in the village. In fact, not once through the years had he been to the McCay house since he agreed to loan them the money to pay the taxes. The McCays had always met him at the bank.

On the rare occasion he did appear in the village, trouble usually wasn't far behind.

A curious group of village folks who recognized the car gathered from afar as Robert Marcoux exited his vehicle wearing his trademark, ill-fitting, white suit with his cowboy hat, accompanied by another man in a better looking suit carrying a glossy, black leather briefcase.

This couldn't be good, a few whispered, making sure not to be overheard. Some of the littlest kids who had no fear, curiously made their way towards the bright shining vehicle, like moths to a light, in awe because cars like this were never seen in the village. They would only have seen one in advertisements or in picture shows, something very few had ever been to see.

"Is this where David and Polly McCay live?" Marcoux asked the closest adult.

When the answer was given in the affirmative he and the other man walked up onto the porch, careful not to step on the second stair, as it was broken, and knocked on the front door.

The door opened almost immediately.

David, in not his Sunday best, stood with a bottle of beer, probably not his first even though it was only a little before noon.

"How can I help you?" he asked, looking at the two men standing there in their suits, squinting from the brightness of the day, and then past them to the curious crowd forming behind them.

"Are you David?" asked Marcoux.

"I am," David replied.

"Is your wife and Jr. here?" Marcoux inquired.

"Nope," David told them, "They're at the old Lanou farm having a picnic," he replied politely.

"Well that's nice," Marcoux said smartly, not really caring if it was or not.

"Let me tell you why I'm here," he continued, when he realized David wasn't going to invite them in. "I'm Robert Marcoux and this is my Lawyer, Howard Greggory."

David tipped his beer bottle to acknowledge the lawyer. He already knew who Robert Marcoux was.

"For the past six years or so," Marcoux continued, "I have been paying your taxes on the old Lanou farm. This year money is a little tighter for me which means that I probably won't be able to pay them. That means that you and your wife and Jr. of course, are going to have to come up with the money." Marcoux finished his statement, euphorically; beyond happy to deliver this type of news, fully knowing from the start six years before that this day would come. Now the trap was sprung.

"Do you think you can do that?" he asked with a smirk on his face, already knowing the answer but looking for David's response.

"I think you already know that we can't," David said.

"Well, what about the money I lent you all these years, can you pay that back?' Marcoux pushed on, antagonizing, knowing full well that if they couldn't pay the taxes for the year they certainly wouldn't be able to pay the larger sum.

David, clearly uncomfortable with the questions being asked and understanding full well where Marcoux was going, answered, "We always understood we owed you money and believed you when you assured us a deal could be reached some day."

"Right," Marcoux said smartly, "you believed, well that's good," he added. "Well, let me tell you what the deal is. You owe me a lot of money, almost twelve thousand dollars, is that correct?" he asked the lawyer standing next to him.

"Close," the lawyer said, "with interest and this year's taxes paid in full, the amount equals eleven thousand, nine hundred and ninety-one dollars," he said in a professional voice, turning the page towards David so that he could see the itemized columns.

"Ohhh," Marcoux cringed in fake agony, letting out a slight whistle, "that is a lot of money, and I want it. I want every last penny of it," he demanded.

"So that's the deal?" David said not so much asking but stating.

"Yup!" Marcoux said short and quickly, "or we could do this a different way," he said teasingly to David.

David knew he was a pawn in the game but the question had to be asked to continue, "And what is the different way?" he asked to Marcoux's enjoyment.

"I'm glad you asked," Marcoux said, happy that David chose to play along.

Robert Marcoux reached towards the lawyer, snapping his fingers a couple times as to say, 'hurry up.' The lawyer produced a thick folder from his leather briefcase and handed it to him. Marcoux held the folder on edge in one hand, waving it towards David as he spoke. "In here, my boy, is the paperwork to sign over the Lanou farm. All you fine folks have to do is to sign on the last page where your names are and we'll call it good."

Marcoux handed the folder to David and asked, "So what do you think you want to do, boy?"

David took the folder. He stared at it for a moment, too long for Marcoux as he chided, "Well boy?"

David answered the only way he could, "We'll get back to you."

Marcoux looked at his lawyer, motioning that it was time to go and then back to David. "Don't wait too long; I don't know how much longer I'm going to feel this generous," he said, letting out a chuckle that sounded like a hyena as he made his way down the stairs with his lawyer in tow.

"Watch out," he said mockingly to the lawyer, pointing to the broken step," I don't want you to fall. We wouldn't want to sue 'em," he said, working himself into a hysterical laughter.

"You're such an ass!" the lawyer said as he threw a fake punch at Marcoux; the 'watch out' comment had made him jump.

"You know what?" Marcoux said bantering back to the lawyer, "that's exactly what my mother said," as the two walked to the car, almost needing to lean on one another to keep from falling over, they were laughing so hard.

Robert Marcoux and the lawyer disappeared into the car. The large white car pulled away fast, creating a cloud of dust, scurrying the little kids who had gathered into their parents' arms. Even the leaves blowing in the breeze seemed to hustle as not to get run over.

The three, David, Polly and Dana spent the fall and most of the winter trying to figure a way to save the farm from Marcoux's clutches.

The only bank they knew was the Ethenburg National Bank, but with Robert Marcoux on the board they surely wouldn't lend them the money, they figured. It didn't matter whether they would or wouldn't anyway. They didn't have the means to pay it back.

Robert Marcoux paid the taxes owed for the year and was relentless with the pressure for the three to make a decision.

So it was that early spring day in the court house with the angry clouds and the dirty snow that Dana would sign over his land, his grandfather's land. The Lanou Estate would become the property of Robert Marcoux in lieu of taxes owed.

Dana was standing in the window when Marcoux's big, usually shiny white car stopped out front of the courthouse. Even his car couldn't resist the dirty snow, as it looked more gray than white in the dusk that was settling on the town.

As usual, Marcoux's mouth could be heard before he was seen as he hollered what he thought to be compliments to the people he passed, which in fact could be deemed darn good insults.

Up the stairs came the footsteps of a heavy man who everyone knew to be Marcoux. He entered the room all smiles. Not a warm smile, but the smile of a conqueror who has beaten his enemy into submission and then taken what riches they had, claiming them as his own.

Dana had left the window and set at the table before he entered the room.

Robert Marcoux acknowledged the lawyer, Frederick Summers. He gave a flick of his hand towards Polly and David that must have meant a hello but reminded Dana of the type of motion that one might have made towards a pesky insect to make it fly away.

The man with the ill-fitting suit sat next to Dana. Too close, as Dana could smell cigar smoke and stale alcohol emitted from his person.

Dana slid away some to distance himself.

Marcoux trained his sight on Dana, his beady eyes boring into him. "You're making the right choice Jr. I just want you to know that you are welcome on my land any time. Hunting, fishing and who knows, I might be able to use you to help hay the fields next year. Hell," Marcoux said, "I might even have you cut some firewood for me after they get done logging. To my knowledge," he continued, "the wood on that land has never been cut. But that will change. I got a crew that's going to start on Monday. I got to do something to make back that money I lent you, you little bastard." Marcoux laughed and slapped Dana on the back.

He turned his attention to the lawyer. "How 'bout it Counsel, you got that paperwork ready? The boys want to play cards tonight and I'm late," he pushed.

"Yes Mr. Marcoux, I'm all set," the lawyer informed him.

"Mr. and Mrs. McCay, why don't you folks take these chairs and then you can have Mr. Thompson set between you two."

It was far from a joyous event but the McCay's managed a faint smile as they moved to their designated seats. They were never called Mr. and Mrs. and it sounded funny to them.

The lawyer spoke his legalese to the three sellers, taking his time to be very thorough explaining what all the forms meant. Marcoux was impatient but bit his tongue for the moment. He certainly was making his presence felt.

Lawyer Summers flipped over the last paper.

"This is where I'm going to need your signatures. I just have to ask you folks, are you doing this of your own free will?" the lawyer asked. When he could see that the three didn't understand what he had just said he started to explain it a different way.

"What that means...."

"All right, all right, all right, already. We know what that means!" Marcoux bellowed, reaching his breaking point of patience.

"Robert," the lawyer lectured, "it is my duty to make sure these folks know what they are signing. If you want to sign that's fine, you can."

"Yes, I do. Show me where so I can leave. I've already told you I was late and you just go rambling on about nothing," Marcoux sputtered.

"Well, we certainly have a difference of opinion," the lawyer shot back. He stood and walked to where Marcoux was sitting, with the paper that needed to be signed.

"You can sign..."

"Yes, I know where to sign," Marcoux interrupted. "You act like this is the first time I ever done this. I've bought and sold more real estate than you have searched titles on," he berated. Marcoux scribbled has name like a man who had signed it many times before. He pushed himself away from the table and stood to leave.

"Is this your dog?" Marcoux asked as he reached down to pet it. The dog raised his lip and growled, backing away at the same time. Nobody in the room had noticed when the black dog with only three legs had entered, but because it was so unusual everybody knew who it belonged to.

"No," replied Dana. "It's Clair Phillips'."

Somebody was making their way up the stairs. It had to be Mr. Phillips. It was known in town, when you saw his dog, Clair was close by.

Clair entered the room slightly out of breath from his long climb. He said hello to the McCay's and Dana and then the lawyer.

"We're kind of busy here," Marcoux said rudely to the old man. Clair acted as if he hadn't heard Marcoux.

"So what's going on here?" Clair asked, looking at Dana.

"Never mind old man, it's none of your business!" Marcoux bellowed.

"Is this what you really want to do?" he asked Dana, not giving time for Dana to answer the first question asked, again acting as if Marcoux wasn't there.

Marcoux hollered at Clair again, "I told you old man, you need to mind your own business." He then turned his irate attention to Dana. "Don't listen to him boy, you and I have a deal. You just sign those papers now!" he demanded.

Clair addressed Dana again, "Is this really what you think your grandfather wanted to happen?"

Dana looked up at this big aging man who had walked into the room with a slight limp, breathing deeply from his climb up the stairs, and a slightly stooped back. What he had noticed first about him was his big, hulking hands. They were hands of someone who had worked all his life eking out a living in all of what northern Vermont had to throw at him. He knew from what his aunt had told him that Clair's land bordered his grandfather's and that they had been friends.

Dana and Polly would occasionally see him as they walked to and from the old homestead to enjoy their picnics. Clair would pass them by in his old Ford pickup with his dog running behind on three legs. Since the dog had fallen out of the truck one time and Clair run over him, he would never get in the truck to ride again but instead chose to run behind, never missing his lost leg.

"No," Dana answered, "this isn't what I want to do."

Now Dana was oblivious to the screaming of Robert Marcoux too, who was making so much noise that all the other people in the court house crowded into the small room to witness the commotion.

Dana continued with Clair, "I owe Mr. Marcoux almost twelve thousand dollars."

"That's right you little double-crossing bastard, you do, so sign those papers," Marcoux screamed, trying to bully Dana.

"Well," Clair said, "if it's ok with your aunt and uncle, I'll loan you the money and you can come work for me. As you can see," Clair continued, "I don't get around as good as I used to. My wife and I could use some young legs and a strong back around the farm. Is that something that would interest you? Do we have a deal?" Clair asked.

Dana looked at Polly and David, excitedly. He already knew how they felt.

All three turned and responded at the same time. "Deal!"

"No deal, no deal!" Marcoux screamed. "We had a deal!" he yelled at the lawyer.

"Robert, I only see one signature and we needed four," the lawyer pointed out.

"Ok then," Clair said, "let's go pick up your clothes. We're late for chores."

Marcoux now was yelling even louder, like a man possessed, threatening that he was going to sue and that the no good kid owed him money and that they had a deal.

Clair turned and spoke on the way out the door to the town lawyer. "If I bring you a check tomorrow could you make sure Mr. Marcoux gets it?" again not directly acknowledging Marcoux.

"It will be my pleasure, Clair," the lawyer said with a big smile.

Clair and Dana made their way down the courthouse stairway and jumped in the old Ford truck that was parked across the street. Clair poked Dana in the shoulder and pointed.

"Look what your dog's up to," he said.

There was Duke, the three-legged black dog, with his hind leg raised, peeing on Robert Marcoux's tire.

Chapter 5

Clair and Dana, with Duke running behind, were out front of the McCay house in minutes. By this time, most of the street lights that were going to light up had, but still Clair was surprised by how brightly his lights on the old Ford truck lit up the street.

It was dinner time, and the smell of maple wood hung in the air thick, as the smoke drifted out of the kitchen stove pipes, wafting up and swirling around the street lights, like a fog had drifted in. Most still cooked dinner on the hundred-year-old wood cook stoves, which also heated the water needed in the house.

Clair, even with the hard life that he and his wife had lived, couldn't help feeling thankful for what little more they had in modern conveniences compared to most in the Mill village. Very few in the village had electric refrigeration, still relying on the ice man, who came around every few days to replenish the melted blocks. Outhouses were the norm, too, although the ones directly on the river used the fast flowing current to flush away their sewage that was clay-piped to the river's edge. Most houses now had town water piped in from Roy Clyde's springs located high up on the mountain named after the town.

"Just grab some old clothes for working and what you're going to wear to school tomorrow and don't be lagging, we are late for chores and that makes the girls ugly," Clair said, referring to his cows that were yet to be milked.

Dana bounded out of the truck and up the steps, making sure to miss the second one that was still broken, through the front door and up the stairs to his room. Pulling the cord to the single light on the ceiling he headed to his dresser but was momentarily confused when he thought back to what Clair had asked him to do. His school clothes and work clothes were one and the same; although they were always clean and neatly folded in his dresser drawer, except for the one shirt that was for holidays or funerals or other occasions, which Aunt Polly kept ironed and hung in the closet.

Clair, waiting outside in his truck, was talking to Duke through his partially rolled down window.

"What do ya think Duke? I don't think I'd like it down here much," Clair said, answering for him. Duke, looking up at Clair, seemed to agree.

Duke's ears perked up. He was looking towards the back of the truck at the two people walking towards them. Clair, looking through his side mirror, could see it was Polly and David as they walked under the dimly lit street light and up to the driver's side window.

"I want to thank you for what you've done, Mr. Phillips," Polly said, adding, "David and I have done what we know how and we could never had come up with the money but we are willing to..."

"You have done a great job," Clair said, politely cutting Polly off.

"You and David have raised a boy to the beginning of manhood and your brother and sister- in- law would be very proud. I didn't know them much, but I did know Dana's grandfather Joe. Joe would have rolled over in his grave to know that his farm went to Robert Marcoux, and had he known his grandson didn't die in that crash I know he wouldn't have done what he did," Clair assured Polly.

"Thank you," Polly said again, as she wiped away a tear with the back of her glove.

David stepped forward to stick his hand through the window to shake hands with Clair and muttered an uncomfortable, "thanks," as well.

"Barbara and I will have you down as soon as we get the boy settled, that is if he ever makes it out of the house," Clair said, looking up at the light in the upstairs bedroom and at his watch.

"I'll go hurry him along," Polly replied with a smile, "and if you were to stop down tomorrow I can have the rest of his belongings packed," she added.

"I'll plan on stopping when I bring the boy to school," Clair replied, adding, "I've got to bring a check to Mr. Summers, too."

Clair watched as the pair headed to the house and smiled as Polly pointed out to David the broken step. David ignored it as he had a hundred times before. They went through the front door just as Dana was coming down with his clothes stuffed in a pillow case.

He made it almost halfway down before he turned and headed back up. "I forgot the light," he called over his shoulder.

"I'll get it," Polly said, "I need to go up and pack the rest of you stuff anyways. You need to hurry. Mr. Phillips is going to leave you here and then you are going to have to find someone else to pay Mr. Marcoux," Polly joked, though her levity had a serious undertone.

"I told Mr. Phillips that he could pick up the rest of your belongings tomorrow and he also said that once you got settled he'd have us down," Polly said.

"I want you to listen to me, Dana," Polly continued, as she put both her hands on his shoulders, slightly surprised she had to look up into his eyes.

In that instant, she couldn't believe that this little one-year-old boy who was brought by the trooper to the house, her brother's son, her own flesh and blood, had grown up so fast and that this day had come so quickly. It was the day that he would be leaving for good, only coming back, hopefully, to visit.

"You need to work hard," she said. "You need to listen. You need to try hard in school. But most of all, you need to be a good person," Polly instructed.

"You need to be respectful to your elders and you need to remember that David and I are always here and you always have a bed if you need it. Can you do these things?" she asked, looking straight into his eyes as she was wiping the tears from hers. "Can you Dana?" Polly urged again.

"I will," Dana promised, getting choked up himself. "I'll make you proud," he added as he reached out to hug his aunt.

"You already have," said Polly, pulling away to allow David to give him a quick hug as he opened the front door.

Dana hustled out the door towards the truck as the door closed behind him. He hesitated, almost turning back, when he heard his aunt let out a loud wail, feeling guilty that he was the cause of it.

Inside Polly stood with her hands over her face, trying to no avail to hold back the tears and catch her breath through her sobs. They got even louder when David put his arms around her, pulling her to him, and said, "You done good Polly, you done damn good."

"You finally ready?" Clair asked, as Dana jumped into the cab of the truck. Clair turned away and looked forward so not to embarrass the boy when he glimpsed his face through the poor lighting, moist with tears.

"Yup," Dana answered, glad that was all he had to say. And with that Clair put the old Ford in gear, glad to leave the Mill village behind. "Come on Duke, let's go home," he directed to his dog.

Dana was both sad and excited that he was leaving the village. It was his home, a home that he had been welcomed in from birth. He was comfortable with the people because he was one of them. He knew it was a place he could always come back to live but, at that moment, somehow knew he never would. It was almost like it had been borrowed time. Now it was time to make it in the other world, a place where very few from the Mill village had ever lived, let alone prospered.

Chapter 6

It seemed odd to Dana to be riding in the direction of the old farm where he and his aunt had walked so many times.

They had walked the road for so many Sundays from early spring to late fall when the weather was good, with Polly carrying the picnic basket when Dana was little, to both of them taking turns, and then as Dana got older, to just Dana.

Every bump in the road brought a flood of memories back and even in the dark the old Ford's headlights brought out the shapes of all the trees and bushes and old guard rails and signs that had become old friends and mile posts with each passing step.

There was the gravel drive to Dana's grandfather's farm coming up, then they passed it by. Dana turned to watch as he seldom had seen it from that angle. In the dark, he really couldn't see much.

"He'll be along," Clair said, thinking that Dana was looking for Duke following the truck. "He's never far behind." Up ahead, Dana could make out lights of a house on the left and a large looming barn silhouetted against the snow and sky.

"We'll go straight to the barn," Clair said. "I had some of the chores done before I went to town, except for the milking and taking care of the young stock. Barbara will come down and show you what you'll have to do. Then you'll be able to do them in the morning before you head off to school," Clair said

The Ford came to a stop outside the barn in front of the milk house door. Dana followed Clair through the door where Clair reached to the right and flicked on the light as he had done a thousand times before. The light illuminated the room, showing its contents.

Against the right-hand wall was a deep, double stainless steel sink that had an assortment of scrub brushes hanging on rusted nails pounded into the wall above the sink. Next to the sink was an electric hot water heater. Across the room in the far left corner, clean shiny milk cans were stacked upside down on a rack.

In the front, left-hand corner of the room was a cement tub that had running water flowing into it dropping from a metal pipe. The water spilled over the edge of the tub onto the floor, making its way to a drain in the middle of the room. The milk house was where the milk was stored in cans and cooled in the cement tub filled with spring water running down off the mountain. The water always ran so as not to freeze in the winter, which also kept the temperature of the tub at 50 degrees or less even on the hottest summer day.

In the center of the small room were two milk cans next to the floor drain where the over flow of water from the cement tub ran. The milk cans had a big white strainer pad rubber banded around the top to filter the raw milk as it was dumped in. Any spilled milk, which would be very little, washed down the drain.

Each can held fifteen gallons of milk and weighed over one hundred pounds when full. When full, a round piece of wax paper was placed over the opening and then a cover was securely popped on using the palm of one's hand to pound it down into place, where it would fit snug and seal properly.

The cans were submersed into the cement tub, which allowed the water to rise just below the sealed cover, cooling the milk so it wouldn't curdle and spoil before it found its way to the local creamery. The milk was picked up daily by a flatbed truck, usually driven by another farmer who ran the routes in between his own chores.

Two swinging doors on the far end of the milk house led to the stables, where a collection of cats and kittens of all sizes and colors were waiting by the door. "We're a couple hours late," Clair said. "The cats are waiting for their milk when we're done. They know not to come in the milk house and if you see one in here swish it out. In the winter," Clair continued, "we need to keep these doors open so the milk house doesn't freeze up. The milk inspector doesn't like it much so if he pulls up, shut them."

Clair and Dana walked through the double milk house doors, entering the stable where Clair turned on another light.

"These are the young stock. You'll be taking care of these," Clair said. Dana could see a collection of about fifteen or sixteen smaller cows and calves all arranged in a line according to size, with their back ends towards them. They were mostly white and black with a couple brown ones mixed in. The animals jostled around in their stalls so they could look behind them to see who had walked in. A couple let out soft moo's as to greet the two. Dana could feel the curious eyes of the animals upon him as if they were asking, 'who are you?'

Dana didn't have much time to study them as Clair never stopped. He reached for a second door, talking as he went.

"Where the young ones are now used to be the horse barn, when we used horses, but now that we don't..." his voice trailed off, not having to finish the obvious. Through the door the pair went where a blast of cool air hit them. Even though they were under cover it felt like they were outside.

Clair continued with the impromptu tour. "This is the hay barn. You can't see much when it's dark."

About fifteen steps and through a third door they walked where a rush of humid, warm air hit them, followed by a chorus of moos. Dana noticed that anywhere there were animals it was warm. "Cows keep it warm," Clair said, as though on cue.

"I know, I know," Clair answered the chorus, "I'm late, I'm sorry!" He flicked on the lights, which made them moo louder and more urgently. Dana was standing at the end of a long row of cows that had their rears to him, much like the young stock.

"How many do you have?" Dana asked.

"Fifteen milkers," Clair answered, continuing down the line where he turned on another switch that filled the stable with the sound of a load engine, drowning out the chorus of moos and making talk nearly impossible.

Dana walked past the running engine. It was about chest high in its own little cubicle. It was loud enough to hurt his ears as he passed. Following Clair to the end of the row of cows, Dana could see three milking machines hanging on hooks behind the cows in the aisle. Two stainless steel pails turned bottom side up were underneath the hanging milking machines.

Clair came over to Dana, got close to his ear and said he'd shut the cover to the milk compressor in a minute, as soon as it heated up, but if it wasn't kept open when it wasn't in use, it would freeze up. Dana watched as Clair reached up and grabbed the first milking machine off its hook and stepped between the first two standing cows. He plugged a rubber hose that was part of the milking machine in to a small valve above the cows' heads then turned it on. This brought the machine to life.

He then slung a leather strap that looked like a belt over the first cow's back. Now squatting down between the cows, Clair fastened the milking machine to the leather strap, suspending it off the ground beneath the cow. Taking a paper towel out of the chest pocket of his coveralls, he wiped the four teats of the first cow clean. Dana watched as Clair expertly grabbed each teat one at a time and squeezed, resulting in a squirt of milk that disappeared into the sawdust. This, Clair explained, signaled to the cow that it was time to start the flow of milk.

Clair then attached the four teat cups to each teat. He watched as Clair attached the other two machines following the same process. When they were all attached, Clair walked over to the milk compressor. He reached up to unlatch a door suspended on the ceiling, allowing it to swing shut to cover the hole and muffle the offensive noise.

"There," Clair said, "now we can hear something. In fact, I think I can hear Barbara coming."

Both looked towards the stable door on the other end of the barn. Duke appeared first, wagging his tail like it had been weeks since he saw anyone, when in reality it had been twenty minutes. Following right behind him was Barbara.

Barbara walked over to them with a half smile on her face. She was about five foot, three inches tall, with the build of a woman who had worked some. She wasn't heavy but not skinny either and clearly handled her weight well. She had thick, gray, long hair pulled back with a kerchief on top of her head, holding it in place. She was dressed in a long wool coat that came to her thighs with work pants tucked into her rubber boots.

"Barbara," Clair said as she stopped in front of them, "this is Dana."

A broad smile now spread across her face as she reached out to shake his hand. Dana, usually a little shy of women, as fifteen-year-old boys can be, reached out to meet her handshake, surprised not only by her strength but how soft and warm her hand was. He instantly felt like he had known her for years.

"You look like your grandfather," Barbara said.

"Thanks," Dana said, not really knowing if that was the way to respond.

"I guess you'll be staying with us for a while," Barbara added.

Dana, now realizing that they were standing alone, as Clair had turned to tend to his cows, responded with a shy smile. "I guess so."

"Well good," Barbara said smiling. She looked him in the eyes and said reassuringly, "It will be okay. Follow me," and she turned and headed for the door. "I'll show you how to take care of the heifers." Not really knowing what a heifer was he followed her out of the stable, through the hay barn where the blast of cold air hit them again, and back into where the young stock were next to the milk house.

Barbara showed Dana how to water the heifers by dipping into the cement tub with a five gallon pail. After filling two of them Dana carried the pails to the front of the animals through the manger. She cautioned him to hold on to the pails as they drank or surely they would spill them if you didn't. Dana asked why the young ones didn't have water bowls like the cows did in the other part where Clair was, to which Barbara replied that this part of the barn was apt to get cool and the water bowls could freeze in the winter. In the summer these animals would be outside.

As Barbara showed Dana his new responsibilities, Clair passed by every few minutes carrying pails of milk which he had emptied from the milking machines and dumped into the stainless steel pails to lug to the milk house. He would then pour the milk through the strainer pads in to the milk cans.

After all the heifers were watered, Barbara showed Dana where to unhitch the trap door which led to the hay barn. She showed him where the light switch was but cautioned him to make sure to shut it off when he was done so as not to be a fire hazard.

"Now, you have sixteen heifers," Barbara reminded Dana. "The first eight get two bales and the other eight get one and a half. They don't need any more, they'll just waste it." They pulled two bales out that had been neatly stacked on edge the summer before and dropped them down the hole which they had climbed up through.

Barbara then showed Dana where Clair, from the morning feeding, had left half a bale which they dropped down as well. The two climbed back down the opening, closing the hole and securing the ladder.

Barbara showed Dana how to cut the twine on the bales and showed him where to put them in the empty grain bag hanging out of the heifers' reach.

She explained that you had to shake each leaf of the hay to break it up, or the animals would pull it through the manger towards them and waste it.

When the hay was fed out, Barbara showed Dana how to hoe the manure into the gutter and explained that if you didn't keep the animals clean and dry they would get sores. In the morning, she told him, he would shovel the gutters and dump them through the hole in the stable where the cows were, but Clair would show him how to do that.

When all the manure was hoed Barbara showed Dana how to take sawdust and bed the heifers. She took a big scoop with the shovel, and, with a smooth swinging motion, spread the sawdust evenly under the heifers. Shouldn't need more than four shovelfuls, she told him. Dana knew what she meant. It was becoming obvious that waste was to be avoided.

"We're finished," she said, looking up at Dana with her big smile. "Think you got it down?" she asked.

Dana assured her he did.

"I hope he does," Clair piped in, coming through the doors with two more pails of milk. "Tomorrow morning I'll show him the rest. Why don't you take him to the house and get him settled in," Clair suggested. He now had both pails balanced on each knee, dumping them into the strainers of the milk cans. "I'll be finished in a half hour or so."

"Great," Barbara said, "I wanted to check on dinner anyways."

Barbara and Dana brushed off the hay chaff and the sawdust and stepped into the milk room to wash their boots before they headed to the house. They stepped out into the cold March night. Barbara reminded him to grab his stuff out of the truck and they made their way across the road the hundred yards or so to the house.

Dana pulled up his collar to protect his face from the wind and was glad that it was only that far. He smiled to himself, thinking about all the animals in the barn, cozy and protected from the elements. The two made it to the house, walked by the front porch and went instead through a door that entered the wood shed. It was still cold but there was no wind.

Barbara showed him where the light was and also the broom for one last cleaning of their pant legs and boots. "We also like to take our boots off here and carry them in. I try my best to keep the barn outside," she told him. "Keep the light on for Clair. He'll want to grab some wood before he comes in."

They entered the kitchen mud room where Barbara showed Dana where to hang his coat and leave his boots.

Dana did as he was instructed and then walked into the kitchen. It was the biggest kitchen Dana had ever seen. On the left was a sink and lots of cupboards. In the corner was a washing machine with big rollers to squeeze the water out of the clothes before they were hung up to dry. Next to the washer was a back door. On the right-hand side of the door was a modern refrigerator and stove. In front of where Dana was standing was a wood cook stove. Dana had never seen one so big and was surprised how black and polished it was. It looked brand new but Dana knew it wasn't. In the middle of the kitchen to the right there was a huge table that must have seated a dozen people.

This is bigger than the whole downstairs of Aunt Polly's house, he thought. "Wow!" he heard himself say. "This is big!"

"It is big," Barbara said, "too big. When Clair was growing up he had five older brothers and they all lived here until they grew up and moved away. His parents lived with us until they passed away a while back."

"Let me show you where your room is and you can take care of your clothes," Barbara offered.

They walked through a doorway to the right of the wood cook stove into another room not quite as big as the kitchen that had six or seven sitting chairs. Hanging on the wall were a dozen or so old pictures of people Dana didn't recognize. There were heavy drapes hung over the windows and a tall, older-looking radio standing on a corner table.

Hugging the wall on the left was a set of stairs that climbed back up over the kitchen. Dana followed Barbara as she started up them. At the top of the stairs Barbara opened a hallway door. When she turned on the light Dana could see five or six other doors lining the hallway.

"We keep this door closed," Barbara said, turning to look at Dana, "to keep the heat downstairs."

She turned immediately to her left and opened the first door. "This is your room. It is also the warmest, as it's right over the kitchen. There is a register over the stove in the corner over there," she pointed to the right. "Before Clair's parents passed away this was our room," she added. "Why don't you take care of your clothes and then come down and I'll show you where the bathroom is and we'll get ready for supper."

"Okay," Dana replied.

Barbara shut the door behind her. Dana looked around, really not believing this whole room was his.

He walked over, parted the heavy curtains and peered out the window to get his bearings. It overlooked the front of the house. One could, if they pressed their face to the glass and looked left, see most of the front of the milk house. Looking straight Dana could probably see most of his grandfather's farm in the daylight, but now all he could see was darkness.

He stepped away from the window and went and sat on the edge of the bed. The bed had a thick multicolored quilt covering it. There were two big fluffy pillows laid across the top near the headboard. *I bet those are soft,* he thought. Not really knowing where to put his clothes he set them in a chair next to the dresser.

I wonder if you can see into the kitchen, he thought.

He walked over to the corner and sure enough, there was the big black shiny wood cook stove below. The heat felt nice as the room was slightly chilly, but that big quilt would keep him warm, he thought.

Dana walked to the door, shut the light out and went downstairs, careful to shut both his bedroom door and the hallway door at the top of the stairs behind him.

He helped Barbara set the table and within a few minutes Clair was through the door with an armload of finely split wood for the cook stove, just as Barbara had predicted.

Supper was a blur. So much had happened in one day.

The courthouse episode with Robert Marcoux seemed like a week ago instead of just a few hours before.

Before Dana was finished supper he could barely keep his eyes open.

"Why don't you go to bed," Barbara suggested to Dana after supper. "Clair is going to have you up at four- thirty tomorrow and that comes quick."

Dana agreed. He was tired, as tired as he had ever been. He washed up and brushed his teeth in the bathroom off the kitchen, said goodnight to Barbara doing the dishes, and walked into the sitting room towards the stairs, where Clair already had his feet up, reading the paper.

"Good night, Clair," he said as he was climbing up the stairs.

"Good night, boy," Clair answered. "I'll be waking you in the morning early and I don't like to wake you twice."

"You won't have to," responded Dana. *I'll make sure he doesn't have to,* Dana thought to himself.

Dana undressed and climbed under the heavy quilt. He laid his head on one of the big pillows.

Yup, he thought, *I was right before. They are comfortable.*

Sleep came quick. Dana drifted in to a deep dream. He could hear voices. They must have been angels. "We have him", one said. "He's here and safe".

"Good!" the other said. "Good!"

CHAPTER 7

Just as both Barbara and Clair had said the evening before, four-thirty did come early. Dana was sound asleep when there was a loud knock on his bedroom door and then the room filled with bright light. "It's time for chores," Clair said, and turned and headed downstairs.

Dana lifted himself up on his elbows, squinting and thinking that light wasn't that bright last night, glancing around the room trying to get his bearings.

Okay, he thought, *now I know where I am.* The temptation to lie back down on the comfortable pillow and pull the heavy quilt back up to his chin spun momentarily through his head but he remembered what he said the night before about Clair not having to wake him twice.

He threw back the quilt and swung his feet to the floor. As he stretched and wiped the sleep from his eyes a shiver went up his body. *It is cool in here,* he thought.

Dana walked over to the chair next to the bureau where he had left his clothes the night before and dug out what he was going to wear to the barn. He pulled his shirt over his head and walked to the window to see if there was any light to be seen. It was pitch black. Not even the moon was out.

Dana couldn't remember the last time he had ever gotten up so early. *Probably never have,* he thought. He walked back to put on his pants. Tomorrow morning, he decided, he would put his socks on first. *The floor is cold!*

Grabbing his socks, Dana walked over and stood on the register. He could see the light coming up from the kitchen. The heat felt good as he balanced on one foot then the other, pulling his socks up.

He could hear and sometimes see Clair fixing the fire below in the wood stove. The sound of a tea kettle whistling filtered up through the register but got fainter as Dana headed to the bedroom door and downstairs, shutting both doors behind him. Rounding the bottom of the stairs and walking through the sitting room, Dana could feel the heat from Clair's fire as he got closer.

Clair was standing at the stove pouring steaming water from the tea kettle into two coffee mugs.

"How do you like your coffee?" Clair asked.

"I've never drank coffee before," Dana replied, not wanting to ask if there was any hot chocolate instead.

"I'll make it like mine then and you can figure out later how you like it," Clair said.

Dana watched as Clair put a spoon and a half of instant coffee in each cup and stirred while he topped it off with cream.

"Yours is on the right, careful it's hot," Clair told him, as he headed for the table with his.

Dana carefully picked up the big mug by the handle and balanced it with his other hand, his fingertips burning on the side of the mug. He followed Clair to the table where Clair had opened a jar filled with homemade donuts.

Dana thought it was good the top of the jar wasn't any smaller, as he watched Clair's big, calloused hand reach in, barely able to get his fingers through, snagging one and pulling it out.

"Help yourself," he said as he took a bite and followed it with a sip from the steaming coffee.

Dana reached in, grabbed a donut and took a bite, following it with a sip of his coffee as Clair had done. The coffee's bitterness must have shown on his face, as Clair commented, "You'll get used to it."

They finished their donuts, put their cups in the sink, and walked to the mud room to put their boots and coats on to go to the barn.

"Barbara found you a pair of old rubber boots to wear so you won't get yours all shit," Clair said. "They probably wouldn't like that in the school house," he added. "Come to think of it you'd probably better wear a different coat too." Clair picked up a couple different coats that were hanging on the coat rack, holding them out so he could compare them to Dana. Finding one to his liking he handed it to him. "Here, try this on, it should fit." Dana slipped into the coat. It fit okay, other than the arms being a little too long. "It works," he said.

Dana slipped on his boots that Barb had found for him. They were both ready to go. Clair looked at his watch before he shut out the light, reaching for the door handle at the same time. "Good," he said, "it's four forty- five. Fifteen minutes is all it should take to get ready."

As they walked through the wood shed door to the outside, Dana was thankful that they had had the coffee and donuts. *It doesn't seem nearly as cold as it was last night with a warm belly,* he thought.

They walked without talking to the milk house. The cold air made Dana's nose feel funny. They entered the milk house as the warm humid air from the animals breathing spilled out into the early morning cold creating a vapor cloud. *That's neat,* thought Dana, just as amused as he was the night before thinking about all the animals keeping warm in the barn, not having to worry about the weather outside.

The milk house looked as it had the night before except the two cans that were on the floor were now in the cement water tank all sealed with their lids on tight. The water, just below the tops of the milk cans, spilled over the edge of the tank onto the floor and into the floor drain. "Sometimes that water freezes on the floor so you have to watch out," Clair warned Dana. "Your rubber boots don't have much traction on ice."

"The first thing we need to do," Clair instructed, "is to get the milk cans ready." Dana grabbed two cans from the six that were stacked on the rack.

Clair opened the cabinet above the cans. "This is where we keep the filters and rubber bands," Clair said, reaching in and grabbing two each. He handed Dana a filter and rubber band and said, "Watch how I do it."

Clair laid the filter over the top of the can and pushed the filter into the can opening so that it created a pocket. When it was deep enough so that milk could be poured into the filter without spilling over the edge of the can he folded the excess edge over the outside of the can and stretched the rubber band over the top of the can to secure the filter. "Just like that," he said. "Now you try it," he said, gesturing towards the second can. Dana placed the filter over the can and with just a little adjusting from Clair did it perfect.

"Barbara already showed you how to take care of the heifers so I'll show you what else you need to do."

Dana followed Clair into the stable where a couple of the young ones mooed as they entered. They turned left towards the hay barn, "Good morning to you too," Clair responded, as he opened the hay barn door. Clair turned on the light that hadn't been turned on the night before. Looking up, Dana could see the peak of the roof and the exposed rafters, probably 80 feet above. He could also see the huge timber beams that made the skeleton of the building.

Dana followed Clair over to a wooden ladder which led to a second floor. "Follow me," Clair said. Clair grunted a few times as they made their way the fifteen feet or so to the second floor.

Clair was rubbing his right knee when Dana stepped up through the hole. "My knee doesn't like that ladder much," he said, sounding a little self conscious as he continued to rub it.

Dana looked around and could see the enormity of the hay barn. Straight ahead and all the way around to the right was hay piled to the roof. Dana could also see where the hay had been taken out of the pile, creating a hole as he had seen the night before when he had fed the heifers.

"When we were done haying last year," Clair said as he watched Dana scan the surroundings, "you couldn't have squeezed another bale in this barn. Where we are standing and all that area where there is no hay," Clair said swinging his arm in a semi circle, "was piled to the roof. You can see how much we fed."

"Ok," Clair said. "We have fifteen milkers and we give a bale to three. So how many bales do we need?" Clair asked.

"Five," answered Dana.

Clair was already grabbing the hay from the pile.

"What we need to do," Clair instructed, "is get the hay over to where we came up and you'll feed it to the cows like you did the heifers. Before I have you do that, I want to grain the cows and have you clean the gutters, which in a few minutes, I'm going to show you how. While you are doing your heifer chores I'll ask you to come back up here to feed the cows. Understand?" Clair asked, as they were lugging the bales over to the spot Clair had pointed out.

"Yup," responded Dana.

"Good," responded Clair as the last bale was stacked, waiting to be fed later. "Let me show you how to clean the gutters, and then I can get milking."

They climbed down the ladder, shut the lights off to the hay barn and turned right into the cows stable where they were met with, as usual, a chorus of moos when the lights were flipped on.

"Yes, I know, things have been a little different with our new boy here," Clair answered them, "but I think he's learning. We'll get back to normal soon."

Turning back to Dana, he continued, "The first thing I want to do is scrape all the shit into the gutter that didn't make it in just like you did last night with Barbara." Clair grabbed the hoe that was leaning against the wall.

"Grab that hoe down there and start on the far end," Clair told Dana, pointing at the hoe further down. They met back in the middle a few minutes later.

"Great," Clair said. "Now let me show you how to clean the gutters."

Walking back to where they had entered were two shovels in the corner. They had long handles and were square-faced.

Clair grabbed them both, handing one to Dana.

"Ok," Clair said, "last thing I need to show you before I set you loose. These shovels fit almost perfectly in the gutters," Clair said as he demonstrated to Dana. The gutters were about a foot deep and traveled the whole distance behind the cows.

"There is a wooden door behind every fifth cow that flips up so that we can push the cow shit down through," Clair said, "but you can't see them now because the gutters are obviously filled. Let me show you what to do."

Clair put his shovel in to the gutter. He shoveled the manure and urine down the gutter a few feet which was about four shovels full, exposing a round ring in a wooded door in the bottom of the gutter.

"Now," Clair said as he stepped out of the gutter, "right here is what you use to pull up the door." He reached over to the wall, and grabbed a steel pipe with a hook attached to the end.

"Just put that hook in the ring like this and pull." As Clair did, the trap door swung open.

Dana looked down in the deep, dark hole that the manure went into. "I don't think I'd like to fall in there," he said, grinning to Clair.

"No I don't suppose you would," Clair responded adding, "that's why you always have to be aware when these doors are open. Now, take your shovel and put it in the gutter about a foot away and just push the shit into the hole. You don't even have to lift it."

Dana did as Clair instructed and pushed the manure through the hole. He could hear it hit a couple seconds later into the darkness below.

"When we're done here you can use that wheel barrow over there," which Clair pointed to the corner where he had gotten the shovels, "and take care of the heifers the same way. Probably be about two and a half loads. Just dump it down this same hole," Clair said pointing to the one he already had opened. They don't have a shit pit under them so we have to wheel it in here."

"A few last things to remember," Clair said, as Dana stopped to listen.

"If you drop your shovel down the hole, you go get it," Clair warned.

"You can be sure," Dana said, "that I won't drop my shovel."

"The second thing is," Clair continued, "when you're standing behind a cow and she lifts her tail, you had better move or you're going to wear it, just like that one down there." Clair pointed a few cows down who was doing her best to fill the gutter.

"I understand," Dana said.

"The last thing," Clair said, " any time you have been in the gutter, go wash your boots before you go in the mangers or hay barn to feed the cows. We don't need to spread diseases by feeding the cows their own shit," Clair explained.

"Got it," Dana said.

"Good, let's get to work. It's already quarter after five and you need to be in the house by seven to shower, eat breakfast, and be ready for school by ten of eight. So you know what to do, right?" Clair asked.

"Yup," Dana answered, arranging in his mind the order for things to be done.

"Good," Clair said, again confident that the boy did know.

The gutters got cleaned in both stables, and when Clair was ready for the cows to be fed, Dana took care of it, as Clair had showed him.

Dana then started the chores that Barbara had showed him the night before. He was finished by six forty-five.

He went into the cow barn where Clair was about half-done milking. He watched as Clair would take off the milking machine from the cow, release the pressure so that he could remove the top of the machine and then dump the steamy, hot, frothy milk into the stainless steel pails.

"I'll do that," Dana said to Clair as Clair was getting ready to grab the handles and lug them to the milk house.

"Don't spill any," Clair said to Dana as he walked towards the milk house with two full buckets.

"I won't," he said over his shoulder, surprised by how heavy they were.

Clair made it look so easy the way he held each pail on his knee, dumping both at the same time. Dana didn't try that. One at a time with both hands would have to do. It was neat to watch the milk stain through into the can, careful not to pour faster than the strainer could handle.

Dana imagined the far-off places, Boston, New York City or any other places the milk might end up, and to think, he was responsible for it.

A couple more trips lugging milk and then it was time to go to the house.

"You did okay this morning," Clair told him. "Now try not to forget in school what you learned today," looking down at Dana with a grin on his face.

"I won't," Dana said flashing a big smile in return.

"I'll be out front by ten of eight to give you a ride to school. Make sure you're ready."

"I will," Dana responded, almost out the door of the cow barn.

What a great morning, he thought. *Getting up at four-thirty doesn't seem so bad after all. It was fun!* as he walked across the road to the house.

He cleaned himself off as he walked into the house just as the grandfather clock in the sitting room was chiming seven bells.

Barb was standing in the kitchen with her hands on her hips. "Well," she asked, "how'd it go?"

"Great!" Dana answered, "Just great!"

"I thought it probably would," she answered back. "Now why don't you grab your clothes, take a shower and I'll make you breakfast."

"Ok," Dana answered as he headed for the stairs.

"You have plenty of time, but there's one thing you have probably figured about Clair," Barbara warned. "He doesn't like to be held up."

"I'm starting to figure that out," Dana replied, as he hustled up to his room.

Dana picked out some clothes from his pile and headed downstairs to the bathroom. He showered and got dressed. When he walked out of the bathroom his breakfast was on the table.

His plate was full of eggs, bacon, and homemade biscuits. *There is no way I can eat all of this,* he thought, but it was gone as quick as he was started.

"Wow!"Barbara said, "Did you have enough? There's a donut if you would like."

"I had all I could eat," Dana responded, but reached for a donut just the same.

They talked small talk about school until Clair pulled out front in the old Ford truck, right at seven-fifty.

"Have a good day in school," Barb wished him as Dana headed for the door. "We'll see you this afternoon."

"Will Clair pick me up or will I walk?" Dana asked as he was slipping on his boots.

"Oh, I imagine he'll pick you up. I would expect him by ten past three so don't …."

"I know," Dana said, cutting Barb off politely." Don't be late." They both were laughing as Dana walked out the door. As Dana jumped in the truck he noticed Duke for the first time this morning. *Where has he been?* he wondered. Dana hadn't seen him since last night.

He asked Clair.

"Funny dog that Duke is," Clair said. "He kinda disappears at night. Always here in the morning, but come nighttime, he's gone. Probably has a girlfriend over the next county," Clair laughed.

The Ford took off towards the village, towards school, with Duke not far behind.

CHAPTER 8

March turned into April and from April showers came May flowers.

Only on the highest peaks or behind some rock ledge where the sun couldn't reach was there any snow left. Where only weeks before the snow was still deep came shoots of rich green grass and colorful flowers, proudly showing their bright yellows, oranges, purples and reds, each vying for the attention of the bumblebees to pollinate them and so help continue life, carrying the pollen from plant to plant. The apple trees all had blossoms, pure white, and their fragrant smell filled the spring air with nature's perfume.

The trees on the hillsides and mountains were in varying stages of light greens to dark, depending on their altitude. The very tallest peaks were still gray, waiting for the latter part of May to reach them with its heat and sunshine.

Nature waits for no one, nor can she be hurried along. Spring happens how it has for millions of years before. Some would swear that this year or that year it was either earlier or later than the years before, but it happens when it happens. On the Phillips farm, spring had sprung and that made it a very busy time of year. For those who didn't keep up it didn't take long to get behind. Clair certainly was going to make sure that didn't happen.

The cows were to be let out to pasture by the fifteenth of May, for at least the daytime. That meant the barbed wire fences had to be mended from all the damage of the heavy snow, and the heaved fence posts that were displaced by the deep frost had to be reset. All the manure that had been pushed down the holes to the pit beneath the barn had to be loaded on to a manure spreader and spread on the hay fields before the grass got too high to fertilize the crops, to ensure the hay barn would be filled to the ceiling again come fall to carry through the winter.

The garden had to be tilled and the peas planted early, with the rest of the vegetables to follow, but always by the last week in May because that was when the threat of frost was over and the sun was hot enough to warm the soil to ensure good seed germination. Dana hadn't realized all that went on in the country. Living in the Mill village kept him isolated from this kind of life. Everybody was certainly busy enough there, but it was different. Life in Mill village revolved around the whistle.

When the whistle blew in the morning everyone went to work. When it blew at noon everyone stopped for lunch and when it blew yet again at five pm everyone left to go home or to the store to grab what was for supper and then soon to bed. The next day it started again the same way, and the next day and next. It was only on Sunday that the whistle didn't blow. Even the people who didn't work at the mill lived around the whistle. In town when the noon time whistle blew, everyone stopped for lunch.

One could be sure that the post office would be busy as well. Most of the people from the mill would come to get their mail as it was the only time they would have the opportunity to do so unless they could come by five-fifteen. Alice, the post mistress, kept it open past five to accommodate the mill crowd.

When the five pm whistle would blow, Rob's market would be overflowing with people from town and the mill as the preparation for supper was underway. The meat counter would be three deep with customers. Rob and two other butchers stood behind the chest-high display case filled with every cut of meat available, with the price per pound sticker showing for each cut. The three would ask the waiting customers, "What can I get ya?" They would then slide open the door from the butcher side and grab what was asked for, slicing the desired amount on the meat slicer and then weighing it out on the large scale that had numbers big enough for the customers to see. It was wrapped, and the purchased amount written on the package, usually figured out in long hand math, to be paid up front.

The store was always buzzing about what went on that day. Smiles and handshakes and people saying hi and wishing one another well were common. The gossip mongers were usually huddled off in a corner or at the end of the meat counter, whispering loudly, pointing and gesturing wildly, swearing all that was being said was the truth. If you didn't believe it, just ask so and so.

The aisles of the store were packed shoulder to cart with everyone politely maneuvering around one another, the littlest kids riding in the carts and the bigger ones hanging on to their mothers' shirts or dresses, pointing at what they wanted or wished for, but being ignored mostly, unless they got in someone's way, for which they were then corrected.

At the front of the store, Danielle, Rob's wife, operated the cash register with its long handle to pull for each sale entered, tallying the purchases. It wasn't like some of the fancier electric ones found in the big cities. The customer would always be asked, "Cash or charge?" The money would exchange hands, change made, and then the correct amount owed would be put in the cash box of the register. If it was charged, the total would be written down in the green box that had the names of the people allowed to charge, to always be paid on Friday unless other arrangements were made.

On the farm there weren't any whistles, but when the wind was right sometimes Dana could hear the mill whistle.

I wonder what Aunt Polly and David are doing right now, he would think to himself, but he knew the answer already. Other than at night, those were the only times he felt a little homesick. He did miss the Sunday picnics that he and his Aunt Polly used to share now that the weather was warmer. He was happy that a few Sundays before, Polly was able to make it down for dinner. David stayed home, but that's what he preferred to do and had always done.

Before they ate, Dana showed Polly his room. He then took her on a tour of the barn and explained all he had learned and the chores he had to do. Polly seemed very happy for him, and Dana thought it was good to see her. After dinner, Dana rode with Clair to take Polly home, with Duke chasing behind.

It seemed normal after saying goodbye that he would be returning to the farm instead of staying in Mill village. Dana liked living on the farm. He liked the responsibility of doing his chores and learning new things. It seemed every day he was taught something or figured out something new.

He also liked Clair and Barbara. They were good, honest, hard-working people. They were fun to talk to and were very knowledgeable. Some of their conversations would be about his mother and grandparents, much like Aunt Polly used to tell about his father. He thirsted for information about his family.

Yes, he knew, Clair and Barbara were good people, and they gave him a connection to his past, something he hadn't experienced much. Talking to them made him feel like it did sometimes when Polly and he would be at his grandfather's homestead and he would be playing among the ruins and the wind would blow just right, making the hair tingle on his arms.

It was on that Sunday Polly had come to dinner, when Dana and Clair were returning to do their chores after dropping her off, when Clair mentioned that, if in a couple weeks, after the mud had dried up from mud season, and if they were able to drive the tractor to it, he had something to show Dana that belonged to his grandfather. Tomorrow was that day, and Dana tingled with excitement.

Chapter 9

It was four-thirty on the dot when Dana awoke. Maybe it was Clair stirring below, but certainly the thought of seeing something of his grandfather's had him excited.

What would it be? he wondered excitedly. Clair had not even so much as given a hint, and Barbara just kept saying she didn't know, followed by that grin of hers, every time Dana would ask.

It's probably just the borders of the farm. That would make sense, Dana thought.

Since he had graduated from the eighth grade and school was over for the summer, and most of the spring work was finished, Dana had hoped to see the land up close. He had never seen what he had inherited. He had only been to the burned-out homestead. From there, Dana could see the hay fields the Rabideau brothers hayed each year for free, as long as they got to keep the hay, which kept the fields from growing up into forests again.

Beyond the fields were the hardwood forests, mostly maple, which made up most of the land.

Towards the back boundary of the property ran the mighty Lords Creek which used to be busy with logs in the spring and smugglers at any time, especially during the rationings of the First and Second World Wars and prohibition in between.

What was striking about the land was a large granite knob that rose uncharacteristically up, seemingly out of nowhere. Granite Hill.

The sheer, bare granite face looked east. It was a formidable piece of stone that rose up five hundred to six hundred feet, and then sloped towards the west. Back when granite was used for foundation stones, coming in from the west was the only way to mine the stone.

Granite Hill, or its face at least, was within the borders of the farm. Because the Lords Creek ran below the face of the cliff, there was a rumor, or legend, that the smugglers of long ago would store their smuggled cargo in the supposed caves of Granite Hill. Beyond the farm's boundaries to the west rose Lowell mountain and Jay peak, where plans for a ski area were being discussed.

Whatever it was he was going to see, chores had to be done first.

Dana dressed quickly. Stopping at his bedroom window as he was in the habit of doing each morning, he could make out the outlines of the westerly mountain ranges as the sun was just thinking about making its appearance from the east. The dark giving way to the light bluish tint that starts every day.

Clair was up and already had the water on.

"Morning," they said in unison.

Dana got the coffee ready for both of them, putting a couple spoons of sugar in his. That made it a little more bearable. The tea kettle seemed to be taking its time this morning. Dana checked to see if the stove was on high. It was.

"So you ready for today?" Clair asked Dana, seeing him fidgeting around the tea pot.

"Yeah," Dana replied, "I'm pretty excited. Could you give me just one clue?" he begged.

"Well," Clair said, "I suppose just one," stopping to think what he could say and not give it away. "Let me see," he continued, pausing again looking at the floor and then back up at Dana. "It's what you are going to be doing in between chores to make money to pay back Barbara and me what we lent you. It also will allow you to make your own money so you'll never have to borrow again to pay your taxes," Clair said.

"How is that?" Dana asked, now confused as ever.

"You'll see," Clair said. "After we get the chores done and everything cleaned up in the barn and get breakfast into us, you'll see."

Dana poured the now steaming water from the kettle that just had started to whistle. He stirred the brown mixture, added the cream, and carried both cups to the table. His mind was a blur. What could it be? Nothing came to mind. He didn't acknowledge Clair's thanks, he was so lost in thought.

He would just have to wait, he concluded as he waited for Clair to pull his donut from the jar to grab one himself. *I'll find out soon enough,* he thought.

Chores went in slow motion. He cleaned the stables in record time but that didn't make the clock hands move any quicker. Time seemed to stand still. The heifers, usually thirsty, seemed to only want to play in the water buckets as Dana put them in front for them to drink. His thoughts wandered, allowing one heifer to spill its water because he didn't have hold of the bucket.

Next week they'll be outside and then they can water and feed themselves, he thought. He swept the water from the manger after the rest had drunk and then hayed them. Dana helped Clair finish milking, lugging the milk to the milk house. They were now shipping over five cans a day and soon expected to be shipping six.

It was spring and the cows had been out to pasture during the day, which helped them give more milk as the new spring grass had more protein and other nutrients than the hay. Next week, because the nights were now warmer and that would allow the pastures to keep up with the cows grazing, they would be allowed out at night.

They let the cows out to pasture when the milking was done. Dana scraped the floor where they all seemed to poop before they made it to the door.

He then spread sawdust to dry everything up while Clair went to the milk house and sealed the cans of milk, storing them in the cement tub.

Dana helped Clair wash the milking machines and buckets and hung them on their rack to dry until the evening milking.

"Done?" Clair asked out of habit, already heading towards the door.

"Yup," Dana said, taking one last look behind him as he went out the door. Duke was there to greet them, back from his nightly visits, his tail wagging a hundred miles an hour. *Someday*, Dana thought, *I'll follow him and figure out where he goes.* But that wasn't really the mystery he was interested in solving right now.

As they made their way across the road to the house Dana could smell the bacon Barbara was frying for breakfast. *It is going to be a beautiful day*, he thought, as he looked up into the bright blue sky through the leaves of the tall sugar maple that bordered the road and corner of the drive.

He checked the mailbox out of habit but knew that Ken Dean, the one-armed mailman, wouldn't be through until after nine.

"Good morning, men," Barbara said as she met them at the kitchen door.

"Morning," they both answered.

"Breakfast ready yet?" Clair kiddingly demanded, picking on Barbara.

"Oh, starting it early today are we?" Barbara countered. "By the time you get washed up probably it will be," she replied good-naturedly.

"I hope it's fit to eat," Clair said, spoiling for more.

"Well after forty-five years of you eating it, it's a little too late to start complaining now," Barbara shot back, raising her fist and shaking it at him as if to threaten him.

Dana loved the way the two bantered.

Every once in a while he would catch Clair patting her rear or pinching at the back of her arm. Barbara would fake alarm or say "ouch!" in an animated way. Clair would just look at her with a straight face, no expression as if he didn't have a clue what was going on. She'd just smile back and make a face. Clearly they loved one another. Dana couldn't ever remember David and Aunt Polly having those moments. It was just different.

"Well," Barbara said to Dana, "I guess you have a big day," turning her attention to him.

"I guess I do," he answered, waiting for Barbara to give something away, but she didn't.

"You better sit down then and I'll feed you both," is all she said.

Barbara opened the refrigerator door and took out the pitcher of milk and put it on the table, followed by the overflowing plate of bacon covered with a towel to keep warm. She walked back to the stove and cracked four eggs one at a time against the large cast iron fry pan that she had used to cook the bacon in. The eggs spattered as they hit the bacon grease. Taking a spoon from the drawer next to the stove she scooped the hot grease over the eggs so they would cook on top. They were done in less than a minute.

Barbara brought the eggs to the table with a tall stack of homemade toast she'd pulled from the oven. "This should get you both started. Let me know if you need another egg," she said to them.

"Oh darn," Barb said, "I'm almost out of butter," as she looked in the fridge on her way back to the stove to make her eggs. "I guess I know what I'm doing this afternoon," she added.

Dana dug into his breakfast. It didn't get any better than this. When he finished his eggs and bacon there was a slice of toast left for each of them, part of their morning ritual.

Barbara would already have on the table a jar of one of her preserves, usually raspberry or strawberry that she had picked the summer before. Dana had learned by watching Clair what to do: Take your spoon and dip it into the jam and drop it on the thick piece of homemade toast that the butter had melted in while it sat in the oven, and spread it evenly to all corners with the back of your spoon. Sometimes it would take two spoonfuls as long as you hadn't licked your spoon in between. It was better than dessert at night! The berries tasted like they had just been picked.

Breakfast was by far Dana's favorite meal.

"If we sit here any longer it's going to be time for lunch," Clair announced as he pushed himself away from the table. Dana had eaten so much he felt sleepy but was over it instantly when Clair spoke. He got up and washed the jam off his face and went to the door to wait for Clair's instructions.

"Well old man, how was breakfast?" Barbara asked, continuing the sparring he had started before.

"It will do for now," he answered, looking at her like he really meant it.

"If you stop back before you head to the woods I'll give you the lunch I've packed for you both," Barbara said.

"Well thank you, my lady," Clair answered, changing his tune. They both smiled, "We'll be sure to do that."

The woods! Dana thought. *At least I know where we're heading.*

"wear your work boots instead of your barn boots," Clair instructed as they got ready in the mud room.

"Under the bench you'll find some work gloves. Grab a couple pair," he added.

"Here," Barbara said to Dana, "give these couple of pieces of leftover bacon to Duke when you go out if you would, please," and handed them to him. Clair and Dana walked out the wood shed door where Duke was waiting. Dana tossed him the first piece of bacon and then the second. Duke looked up for the third. "That's all, boy," Dana told him, and held out his empty hands to show him.

Dana followed Clair to the workshop.

"We're going to get the John Deere out," Clair said, "so slide open the door after I unlock it."

Clair went inside the shop. Dana could hear Clair fooling with the chain that held the door shut.

"Ok," came the muffled order.

Dana slid the door along its track and exposed that side of the shop to the morning sun. The green John Deere, with its faded paint, was parked in front. It was already hitched to a utility trailer made out of an old manure spreader.

"We've got to load a couple things in the trailer," Clair said. "Grab that toolbox over there. Make sure the cover is closed tight or you're going to pick them all up," Clair advised.

Dana checked the latch and reached to pick it up. He tried with one hand and then the other and then with both. *Man*! he thought. *This is heavy*! Dana swung it up into the back of the trailer and pushed it far enough forward so it wouldn't fall out. Clair was coming up behind carrying a large box with little caps on top. "What's that?" Dana asked.

"It's a marine battery," Clair answered. "There's another one on the work bench under the window. Grab it but be careful. It's heavy and it has acid in it that will burn you if you tilt it too much."

"Should I wear my gloves?"

"Good idea to," Clair answered back.

Clair threw in a couple long chains, two red five-gallon cans of diesel and two different length hand saws.

"What's this all for?" Dana asked, looking for any clue.

"You'll see," is all Clair would answer. "Ok," he declared, "I think we have everything. Why don't you go grab our lunch and I'll pick you up."

"Ok," Dana said, and trotted towards the house.

He couldn't believe that the time had finally come to see what Clair and Barbara were keeping secret. He was nervous, excited and eager.

"Have fun," Barbara said as she handed Dana a huge basket that seemed as heavy as the tool box he had loaded. "Be careful with that," she added, "there's glass in there."

Dana laid the basket over the side of the trailer and went to climb in the back.

"Up here," Clair said, motioning to him to climb up on the left hand side of the tractor.

Dana hoisted himself up and braced himself against the tire fender to steady him.

"I can point things out to you," Clair said, leaning closer so that he could be heard over the noise of the engine. Clair revved the throttle a little more and let off the brake as he slowly moved the hand clutch forward to engage the tractor in gear.

The John Deere started slowly and smoothly, with a big puff of black smoke coming out the upright exhaust. It picked up speed as the clutch fully engaged. Dana looked back to see where Duke was. Barbara was waving from the porch, smiling broadly as she always did. He tossed a quick wave back, not quite sure how much he wanted to let go of the tractor yet. They were on their way.

They slowed only to make sure there was nothing coming from the left and continued towards town. Clair pulled the clutch back to disengage, grabbed another gear and engaged it again, this time cutting back the throttle as the higher gear allowed the tractor to go faster.

"This is the next thing I'm going to teach you," Clair said, motioning towards the tractor, obviously meaning that he would teach him how to drive it. "Depending how you do today, maybe on the way home," he added. Dana thought that whatever happened today would be easier than driving this tractor. There seemed to be a few more moving parts than what made him comfortable.

They were about halfway to his grandfather's homestead driveway when they met Ken Dean, the mailman. They all waved at one another. Dana thought it was amazing how even with one arm he could still deliver the mail. Ken had lost the other in World War Two.

Clair cut the throttle on the tractor and disengaged the clutch. He turned left and crossed the road, coasting up to a barbed wire gate.

"I'll have you open the gate and after I drive through it you need to close it," Clair said. "We don't ever leave a gate open."

Dana jumped down and undid the top wire and pulled open the barbed wire gate to let the tractor through. He closed it after as

Clair had asked, climbing back up to his perch on the tractor. He was going to ask why they wouldn't leave it open, seeing how they would be coming back through, but Clair spoke before he could ask.

"That gate and this road are the property line between your grandfather's, I mean, your farm," Clair said, correcting himself, "and my farm. We'll follow it for a little ways, then cut onto your property," he said.

They travelled for a quarter mile or so and stopped at another gate on the right. Dana jumped off without being told and let the tractor through again, then closed it. He pet Duke quickly before he jumped back on the tractor.

"Like I explained a few minutes ago," Clair said," we are now on your land." It was becoming clearer to Dana every time Clair said, "yours." This was his land. Thanks to Clair and Barbara, this was his land. They continued west along the edge of a hayfield, following a road that led into the forest.

Dana noticed that the road was bringing them closer to Granite Hill, but lost sight of it as soon as they got in the woods. The forest was thick. Even though the leaves were new, they had already started to form a canopy over the road.

"Are these maples?" Dana asked, pointing at the trees.

"Mostly," Clair answered, "but there are others as well that we will probably end up thinning out."

Duke had now gone ahead of the tractor, as if he knew the way. They travelled for a few more minutes, going slow. Clair seemed more interested in the trees than he did the road. Dana looked ahead and could see it getting lighter, like a clearing was approaching. He could hear something, but couldn't quite figure out what it was. Slowly the tractor crawled, the engine at an idle. The noise got louder.

As Dana thought, the tractor pulled into a wide clearing. Before them was Granite Hill. It was as massive as anything Dana had ever seen. It surprised him that it was so large and that they were so close to it. The sun was shimmering off the flat surfaces of its face. It seemed like it reached the clouds. It looked so high! Almost like one of those skyscrapers in New York City!

Dana now understood what the noise was he had heard driving up to the clearing.

In front of him was a waterfall on Lords Creek, which ran at the foot of Granite Hill. It cascaded over a twelve foot drop, crashing into the rocks below, sending up spray and white foam, flowing into a long pool. Not only did it look powerful, it sounded powerful too.

Awesome! was all that came to Dana's mind. *Just awesome!*

The canopy had stripped away and they were now in a clearing probably fifty yards wide and a couple hundred yards long. Clair had stopped the tractor and was watching Dana's expression. He had a smile as big as Dana's as he watched. He remembered when he was about Dana's age, maybe a little younger, and seeing this for the first time, wondering if he had looked the same way. It *was* impressive.

Clair put the tractor in gear and turned to the right as Dana stared at the granite wall and waterfall. Clair continued another hundred yards as Dana followed the path of the river.

What a huge swimming hole, he thought. *I could even dive off some of the rocks that protrude towards the middle. It certainly looks deep enough. It's probably a great place to fish too,* he imagined. Dana pulled his gaze away from the river. What was that ahead of them? It was a large structure of something covered with a black heavy canvas. Clair pulled up beside it and shut the tractor off. It was the height of the tractor.

"What's underneath the canvas?" Dana asked curiously.

"This, my boy, is what is going to make you money," Clair answered.

Dana had to admit to himself; this certainly hadn't lived up to the suspense he had felt for the last couple weeks. After seeing what he had just seen, how would this thing ever compare, and what was it?

"Help me get the canvas off," Clair said. "We'll flip it over this way," motioning away from the river, "and then we can fold it up." As they pulled the canvas away the mysterious object started to take shape. The first part appeared to be a large box, probably six feet tall and five feet long. It had writing on the side that said, Property of the U.S. Government.

"What is it?" Dana asked again, more curious after seeing the writing than when he saw it first.

"Let's get it all uncovered and I'll show you," Clair answered.

Along each side was a platform that allowed each person to climb up onto opposite sides of one another, and it appeared to run the length of the machine hidden by the canvas. Next, a long piston appeared, as they worked to strip away more of the canvas. Then a long I-beam with ribs pointing up that looked like it would keep something balanced on the beam.

Next was a huge circular saw blade with menacing teeth, probably sharp enough to cut the contraption in half.

"Watch that saw blade," Clair warned, "I don't want to rip the canvas....or get cut," he added. Finally the last part of the canvas was off, revealing a large triangular wedge type thing that was positioned on the very end of the I-beam. The two pulled the heavy canvas up towards the woods and started to fold it up. Dana couldn't take his eyes off of this huge machine. It had to be twenty-five feet long. It ran parallel to the river.

"Pay attention," scolded Clair "or I'll never get a chance to explain what it does."

Dana snapped back to attention and in a couple minutes the canvas was neatly folded.

"Follow me," Clair said, walking back towards the machine.

"This, Dana," Clair started, "is something that your grandfather built but never got a chance to use. It is a wood processor that cuts firewood from full- length logs."

"Neat," Dana said, "but how?"

"Come up here," Clair motioned to Dana, "and I'll show ya." They climbed up a few stairs and stood on the same side.

"You see this big box?" Clair asked, not stopping for an answer. "This is a diesel generator that your grandfather bought at a government auction. It was going to be used in the war," he said, referring to World War Two. "Well they never used it. It was brand new. He took this," pointing at the generator, "and he got this piston from one of their old dump trucks," pointing as he spoke, "and hooked them together with a big hydraulic pump that's under the box as well," as he tapped the large structure.

"So what happens is you stack your logs up onto that landing over there," Clair explained, pointing over the machine towards a flat spot between the river and the machine on which they were standing.

"Then you roll a log onto those two forks," pointing over the machine to the ground at two pieces of curved metal about four feet apart with the ends laid flush against the ground. "The forks have a piston on them that picks up the log and dumps it on to this I- beam track in front of us. These ribs hold the log from falling off," he said, touching them for emphasis.

Clair was excited as he spoke, watching to make sure Dana was following what he said. When he saw that Dana was, he continued. "The piston bumps up to the end of the log," he said pointing at the end towards the generator, "and pushes the log underneath this saw blade. The saw blade comes down and cuts the log any length you need by pulling this lever right here," Clair said, reaching over and touching it so that Dana could see.

"The piston continues to push the log into the splitter head on the end after it's cut and splits it into quarters. And you see how it just falls underneath?" Clair asked, looking right at Dana. "Well that's where you would put your trailer so you don't even have to load it. The wood just falls in. It's all run by hydraulics, powered by the generator and it's all controlled by pushing these buttons on this cord," Clair said, holding up the cord.

Dana looked it all over. "You never have to touch the wood except to pull the log up to the gate?" Dana asked, but it was really a statement.

"That's right," Clair answered, already as excited as Dana was becoming.

"Does it still work?" Dana asked.

"It should," answered Clair. "We have the batteries and the diesel fuel to find out. I've checked on it over the years and kept it covered, so I don't know why it wouldn't," Clair said.

"So," said Dana, "What do we have to do to find out?"

"Well, let's hook everything up and see what happens," Clair answered.

The two men went to work, with Dana following Clair's lead.

"We need to get the batteries hitched up first,"" Clair directed. "We'll need the tools too. I'll open the cover to the generator if you grab them." Dana stepped off the platform and climbed into the back of the trailer. He put on his gloves and slid the batteries and toolbox to the end and jumped down off the trailer.

The batteries didn't seem near as heavy as they did before, as he placed the first one on the platform and then the second. He then grabbed the tool box and swung it up. Clair already had the cover open and the first battery in place. Dana watched over Clair's shoulder as Clair hooked up the first battery. "Why don't you grab the diesel and dump it in that filler pipe," Clair instructed, pointing to the pipe. Dana grabbed both of the cans from the back off the trailer and emptied them into the fuel tank.

Clair had both batteries connected and the cover closed by the time he was finished. It hadn't even taken twenty minutes to get it ready to try. "Here goes nothing," Clair said, looking at Dana with his fingers crossed. He turned the key to the "on" position, pulled the choke and pushed the start button. The old motor turned over like it was brand new. With a puff of black smoke the generator fired up with a roar. Dana and Clair gave each other a thumbs up.

"Let's try the rest of the hydraulics," Clair hollered over the noise of the generator. They climbed onto the river side of the platform and walked down to where the control cord hung. Clair showed Dana how to operate the buttons. Dana pushed the top button and the two forks swung up just like they were dumping a log onto the I-beam.

Dana pushed the second and the piston moved towards them as if it was pushing a log.

Dana pushed the third button and the saw blade spin to life. He reached up and grabbed the long handle to cut the imaginary log and was surprised by how effortlessly the saw blade pulled down.

"Do it all again," Clair hollered over the noise, pointing at the cord in Dana's hand, "and I'll check for leaks." Clair checked for leaks as Dana tried everything again. There were none. Everything worked.

Clair took his finger and drew it along his neck to tell Dana that he was going to shut it down. Dana followed to watch how. Clair looked at the gauges on the generator and seemed happy with what he saw. He turned the key to the "off" position and the generator fell silent. Clair and Dana stood shoulder to shoulder, marveling at the creation.

"Your grandfather was a pretty clever man," Clair said matter-of-factly.

Dana was as proud of his grandfather as anyone could ever be, though he had never met him. He heard himself, thinking in his mind, as if he was talking to him, "I won't let you down. I will make this happen."

It was only when Clair put his arm around him for the first time ever, and said, "I know you won't, Dana. I have faith in you," that he realized he had been speaking out loud.

Chapter 10

The two stood silently for a moment. Clair was the first to speak.

"This didn't take near as long as I thought it would," Clair said. "What do ya think? Why don't we look around and see if we can find some broken limbs big enough to try this thing out?"

"For real?" Dana asked excitedly, "Really? I'd like to!"

"First things first,"" Clair responded. "Let's bring the trailer around and unhitch it underneath where the wood will drop. Might as well bring what we split home."

"We can leave the toolbox and the fuel cans right where they are for now but we need to grab the chains and saws and lunch basket out of the back. Why don't you jump up there and grab everything and bring it to the back."

Dana jumped up and grabbed everything as Clair had asked. Clair grabbed the chains and saws and set them off to the side.

"We'll put these back on the tractor after we unhitch the trailer. We'll need them in a little bit. If you want, you can set the lunch over in the shade," Clair said, pointing off twenty feet or so. Clair came around the side of the trailer and headed for the tractor. Dana grabbed the basket to do as he was instructed.

Dana noticed that Clair was favoring his right knee again. It was the same one that he rubbed when he went up the ladder to the hay barn. Dana had noticed him limping in the morning until he limbered up and always after chores. *I'll have to make sure that I get ahead of him to grab anything heavy,* Dana thought, *he certainly won't ask me to.*

Clair climbed up on the tractor and started it. He pulled around the bottom of the hill and backed it up underneath the wedge that split the wood. Dana jogged over after placing the lunch near the wood line, telling Clair, "I'll get it," referring to the jack on the trailer.

Clair drove the tractor back around up top and shut it off by the chains. He was off and wrapping the chains around the three point hitch arms and hanging up the saws when Dana came back around. Dana watched as Clair finished and stood up.

"Before we get started, let me give you some history, thoughts and instruction." Clair began.

"When your grandfather built this fifteen years ago or so they were still doing the log drives down this river," Clair explained, as he waved and half-turned towards the water to make his point.

"The waterfall used to slow the logs down and the men who drove the logs used to have to work hard to get the ones that hung up in the rocks free; lots of times too hard. By the time they did get them freed up, the drivers were too far behind the main pile of logs. So most times, unless it was quick, they would just leave them. So your grandfather thought, why let them just sit there and rot? He also told me," Clair explained, "that if he could buy the logs before they got to the mill he could buy them for the same price or maybe a little cheaper than the mill would pay. The drivers could just roll them off to the side of the river, your grandfather could pile them up, and it would work for everyone" Clair explained. "That's why he built it here," he added.

"But why wouldn't he just cut these trees?" Dana asked, "there are thousands of them," he said, turning as Clair had when he waved to the river.

"I'm glad you asked," Clair said proud that the boy was listening so intently. "Your grandfather, to my knowledge, had never cut a healthy sugar maple. He didn't even tap them to make maple syrup, although he wasn't against it. The only time he would ever cut one was if it had gone past its prime, was diseased or got damaged by the wind or lightning. He had always told me, you can cut enough wood in this forest that has fallen or died, or trees other than maples that took their sunlight, to supply enough wood forever without cutting a healthy sugar maple. And with this many trees, he's right," Clair exclaimed.

"As far as I know," he continued, "this forest is the same way it was when the white man came. It has never been cut, only the ones that needed to be."

"Wow!" Dana said. He remembered that Robert Marcoux had said the same thing a few months back and how anxious he seemed to want to log it off. He now understood even more what Clair and Barbara had done for him....and for his grandfather.

"So what do you think?" Clair asked, looking at Dana. "Do we continue the wishes of your grandfather, or do we do something totally different?"

Before the words had time to leave Clair's lips, Dana responded, "We do exactly as he had wished."

"Good boy!" Clair replied, adding, "He'd be proud."

"So I think what we ought to do for now," Clair continued, "is head out the road we came in on and find some smaller broken limbs closer to the road. I saw some when we were riding in. Without a chain saw and a wood peavey we will have a tough time with the bigger ones," he added.

"What's a peavey?" Dana asked.

"That's what you use to roll logs with. I'll show you one when we get back to the shop," Clair said, adding disgustedly, "like an idiot, I didn't think to bring them." Clair climbed back on the tractor and Dana followed.

"Have you seen Duke?" Dana asked just before Clair started the tractor.

"I wouldn't worry too much about that dog," Clair said, "he has a mind of his own." Clair put the tractor in gear. Dana watched closer how he worked the clutch. *I bet I could drive this,* he thought to himself, *as long as Clair showed me.*

Clair pulled up closer to the waterfall. This time Dana could get a better look. With the granite wall behind and the sun reflecting off its face he had to stare almost uncomfortably straight up to see its top. *Massive!* he thought, *just massive!* And the noise the waterfall made tumbling over the rocks; the only time Dana had heard anything so loud and powerful was when he once stood next to the railroad tracks as the Canadian Pacific train rushed by with four locomotives pulling almost a hundred cars.

The road took them out the way they came in, away from the falls and underneath the cool canopy of the old growth maples. Clair was looking from side to side for just the right branch. "There!" he said as he disengaged the clutch. "We'll hook on to that one," pointing to a branch that had broken off one of the maples but was still lodged up against it, probably twenty feet off the road.

"What I'll do," Clair said, looking at Dana, "is back up to it. We'll take the chain and yank it out. It should come easy." Clair pulled up past the limb and put the tractor in reverse.

"Why don't you jump down and walk behind the tractor," Clair asked Dana. "I don't want to get hung up on a rock," he explained. Dana jumped down and was surprised that the ferns growing in the maples were almost waist high. Clair worked the clutch and maneuvered to within fifteen feet or so, setting the parking brake so the tractor would stay.

"Let me show you how to hitch the chain to skid logs," he told Dana.

Clair unwound the chain from the three point hitch. "You see how the chain has two different types of hooks on each end?" he asked Dana, holding them both up. "This one," Clair said, holding up the hook, "when you hitch it to the chain, locks in so the chain won't slide through," as he ran the chain through the frame of the tractor and hitched the hook into the chain.

"Now this one," Clair said, holding up the other hook, "has a wider bite." He demonstrated how the hook would slide along the chain. "It will tighten up when you wrap it around the tree and pull the slack." Dana watched, always eager to learn, and could see the difference in the ends.

"Let's hitch it to that big limb and I'll show ya," Clair said eagerly.

They walked the few steps to the tree. "You always want to hook underneath when the log is still stuck in the tree," he said, "just like this." Clair reached around the limb with the chain and laid the chain through the hook.

"See how it can slide?" he showed Dana as he pulled the slack of the chain. Dana nodded.

The tree limb was about a foot thick on the smaller end.

"Ok," Clair continued, "I'm going to slowly pull the slack up with the tractor. What I want you do is stand closer to the tractor and hold the chain so we don't lose our slack until I can tighten it, because the hook around the tree can come loose unless there is pressure on the chain. Once the chain's tight, step away over there and you can follow the limb out to the road. Watch how the limb spins because we hitched the chain underneath, got that?" Clair asked looking at Dana to make sure he did.

"Yup," Dana answered as he usually did.

Clair climbed back on the John Deere and put the tractor into first gear, low range and eased the clutch, giving it a little more throttle. Dana held the chain until it tightened, then stepped away as he had been instructed. The tree limb lifted up and rolled with a crash as it dislodged from the big maple. There were a few smaller limbs still attached. Dana was surprised that it came so easy. He followed it out through the ferns and back into the road.

Clair stopped the tractor again, set the break and climbed down. "I want to show you one last thing." he said. "We don't need this limb dragging twenty feet behind us so we need to shorten it up. What I want you to do to unhitch this grab hook that we first hitched to the tractor. When I back up pull the slack through the frame and hitch the hook closer to the tree, shortening the chain. Make sense?" he asked Dana.

"Yup," Dana answered.

Clair jumped back on and carefully backed up, with Dana pulling the slack, hitching closer to the tree. Clair waved his arm for Dana to join him on the tractor. When he was settled, Clair headed for the wood processor.

"I'll pull up to the landing and you can unhitch it," he said adding, "then we'll go get another."

A couple more hours later and they had managed to pull up another three limbs of varying sizes. Clair never had to get off the tractor; Dana had caught on quickly, as he usually did. After Dana unhitched the last one, Clair pulled the tractor around and shut it off.

"What do you think boy, ya hungry?"

"Kind of," replied Dana.

"Why don't you grab that basket and we'll have lunch down by the river," Clair suggested.

"Sounds good," Dana answered, and walked up to grab it. He joined Clair, who had already picked a spot with a large flat rock that acted as a table. "Set it right up here," Clair said, patting the rock, "and we'll see what she made us." Clair opened up the basket and dug in. Dana looked over Clair's shoulder, peering in, curious too.

"Looks like we have some chicken sandwiches," Clair announced as he unwrapped one from the wax paper. "Got some hard-boiled eggs, too." Dana had guessed the chicken part. That's what they had for supper the night before and saw there was plenty left over, even though he had eaten until he thought he'd burst.

"Oh, and she has us some apple pie, too, for dessert," Clair added as gleeful as a kid at Christmas.

Out of all the things that Dana had learned about farm life; you ate good. He was always busy doing fun things. There wasn't time to be bored. It really didn't seem like work. It's just what you did. It certainly built up his appetite.

Barbara had made some iced tea to go with lunch. Eating his sandwich and washing it down with the tea brought back memories of when he and Aunt Polly did the same thing for so many years as he was growing up. How many times had he played among the old cellar holes and envisioned what it would be like if his parents and grandfather were still alive?

Now it was him and Clair and Barbara, and of course Aunt Polly and David. Not only was he the owner of this land, his grandfather's land, he was its protector. Now he was going to be able to pay back what Clair and Barbara had loaned him. And pay his own taxes too. All because of what his grandfather had built.

Certainly his grandfather hadn't known when he built this machine that someday his grandson would use it to save their land from being destroyed. This machine gave Dana the means to do that. In a way, they were doing it together.

He thought how lucky he was to have met Clair and Barbara, and so was his grandfather. What would have happened had Clair not shown up at that moment? Just the thought sent a shiver through Dana's body. What would he have done without them? To think about Robert Marcoux in here with a bunch of tractors cutting this whole forest, decimating in weeks what took thousands of years to grow, made Dana cringe.

Dana remembered vividly Marcoux's words about having a crew waiting to start, and how greedy and eager he seemed to want to make this all disappear. Did people like that even appreciate the beauty of something like Granite Hill? Would they have been in awe like he was a few hours before? What about the river with its waterfall and history? Is their life only about greed and money? Are they able to feel, to appreciate anything? Dana vowed to himself that as long as he was able, this land would remain as his grandfather had wished, and Clair and Barbara's as well.

"You're awful quiet over there," Clair said, breaking up Dana's thoughts, "everything ok?"

"Yeah," Dana answered, "I was just thinking."

"I was too," Clair said.

"About what?" Dana asked.

"I was thinking what a horse's ass I am for not bringing those peaveys," Clair said angrily. "We're going to have a hell of a time rolling these limbs without it." Dana hadn't given it much thought, and really didn't know how a peavey would make it better, but agreed with Clair anyway.

"I think we had better think of a strategy to keep you supplied with wood, too," Clair said. "I think we might have to invest in a chainsaw. They have newer ones that are a lot lighter. Only takes one person to run them, not two."

"Really?" Dana asked, excited about the thought of learning how to run one. "How much do they cost?"

"Not sure," Clair said, "but after we're through here today we might run into town to find out."

Dana, finished with his lunch, surveyed their small pile of limbs. *How would they get those limbs up there?* he wondered.

The two were thinking about the same thing, Dana realized, when Clair said, “I think for today we should take that closest one, saw off those smaller limbs with the limb saw and roll it up there however we can and call it a day. That would give us a chance to try this machine out and then we could come back tomorrow properly equipped,” he added.

“Sounds good to me,” Dana replied, excited about seeing how the machine handled wood. They picked up the basket and Dana went to put it up where the tools and fuel cans were. He heard Clair sawing the limbs with the limb saw. It only took him a couple minutes and he had what he wanted done.

“I think what we need to do,” Clair said, “is to hitch both these chains on each end of the log and run them under the processor, where I’ll hitch on the other side with the tractor and pull the log to the machine. I wouldn’t normally do that but I’m as excited as you to see this work,” he said, grinning at Dana.

They hitched up the chains to the log and ran them under the machine. Clair pulled the tractor around and Dana hitched the chains to the draw bar.

“Stand up there and tell me when it’s up to the forks,” Clair instructed. Dana climbed up to his vantage point. Clair pulled ahead and Dana waved when the log was at the forks. Dana unhitched the chains and pulled them out through on the tractor side.

“Perfect,” Clair said, “but not what I want to do that ever again,” after he had gotten off the tractor, still disgusted with himself. “Let’s give it a whirl and see if this baby will work.”

Dana was excited.

“Remember how I started it?” Clair asked.

“Yup,” Dana said.

"Well then, go start it," Clair instructed. Dana turned and headed for the switch. He pulled out the choke and hit the start button. Nothing happen. He hit the button again. Still nothing. He started to feel panicky. Had they broke it before they had a trial run?

"Turn the key on," Clair hollered over. He was observing from where the large circular saw was.

"Oh," Dana said, feeling embarrassed. He turned the key, hit the start button and the machine, like before, roared to life. Dana pushed in the choke and joined Clair on the platform.

Clair waved his hand at Dana as if to say, 'it's all yours.' Dana held the control box in his hand. He was nervous. He pushed the button to raise the log. It easily picked it up and deposited it onto the I-beam.

Dana pushed the second button and the piston extended until it met the log and pushed it towards the saw. He stopped when Clair tapped him on the shoulder and held his hand for the control. Had he done something wrong? he wondered.

Clair could see what he was thinking and shook his head no and held up his finger as to say 'watch.' Clair pushed the second button until the jagged edge of the log went a few inches past the saw. Clair then pushed the third button and the saw blade whirled to life. He motioned to Dana to pull the handle down. Dana pulled the handle down to the log. The saw buzzed through like it wasn't even there, squaring up the end that would soon meet the triangular splitting head.

Clair gave Dana back the control and waved his hand to continue. Dana pushed the second button until Clair stopped him again. Clair pointed to a mark on the side of the rail that was numbered 12 through 24. The end of the log was on 20. Clair motioned for Dana to cut.

That's twenty inches, Dana thought. *That's how you know what length to cut the wood at. Neat!*

Dana hit the saw button and pulled the lever where it cut just as smooth as before.

This works great, Dana thought.

Dana pushed the piston button again until he hit his mark and dropped the saw again. He repeated it and this time the first piece of wood had reached the triangular end which was to split the wood.

Dana watched as the piston easily pushed the twenty inch chunk of wood into the triangular wedge and couldn't help but to smile when the wood split into four pieces and dropped, as it was intended, to the trailer below.

This isn't work, it's fun, Dana thought. He continued the sawing and splitting until the piston reached the saw and would go no more. *That,* Dana figured out, *is so you can't cut into the piston.* Dana looked at Clair and Clair drew his finger across his neck. Dana made his way to the control panel and turned the key to shut it down.

"That is so neat," he said to Clair after the machine quieted down.

"It works well," Clair said, "better than I expected."

"Tomorrow we'll do some more. I want to show you some things to watch for like checking the oil and stuff, but that's tomorrow. Let's cover this up and pick our stuff up," Clair said. "We'll go to town before we start our chores." They covered the machine, hooked on the trailer and were headed towards home in a few minutes.

On the way out Dana was looking on both sides of the road for downed trees, just as Clair had on the way in. He caught some motion out of the corner of his eye. There was Duke. *Crazy dog,* Dana thought. *Clair was right; he certainly has a mind of his own. We haven't seen him all day and the minute we're headed for home, there he is.*

CHAPTER 11

Duke led the way through the gates as Dana opened and closed them for Clair, as they made their way back to the farm.

"Might as well leave everything in there except the lunch basket," Clair said, after he backed the tractor and trailer into the workshop, adding, "what little wood that's in there can be seed for tomorrow." Dana reached over the edge of the trailer and grabbed the basket, smiling to himself at the small pile of his new endeavor on the floor where it had fallen from the splitter.

Going to take a heck of a lot more than that, he thought, *to save the farm.*

Clair was walking back towards the tractor with two wooden tools that looked like baseball bats with hooks on them. *Those must be the peaveys that Clair talked about,* Dana thought, which Clair confirmed.

After putting one in the trailer, Clair showed Dana how you would drive the peavey towards the log, and the hook would grapple the wood, which then you could use the leverage of the handle to roll the log. Dana paid attention as best he could without actually having a log there, and nodded when Clair was finished. His thoughts were more on going to town and seeing, and hopefully buying, a chainsaw.

Clair put the peavey in back of the trailer with the other one and looked at his watch.

"Let's take the basket to Barbara and let her know what we're up to. Maybe she'll want to ride into town with us," Clair said. Dana nodded and turned to walk out of the shop.

"Slide that door shut and I'll latch it," Clair called after him.

Dana set the basket down and slid the door shut. He heard Clair through the door latching the chain used to secure it. He picked up the basket and waited for Clair. As they walked towards the house Barbara walked out onto the porch.

"Everything go all right?" she asked.

"Went fine," Clair answered, "but I forgot the peavey. Getting forgetful in my old age," he said, still disgusted. She held out her hand to Dana to take the basket and continued, "Well I thought something was up when I saw the small load you guys brought home. That will get us through about a half a day this winter," she picked.

Clair agreed, taking the picking well and added, "The processor worked great but we're going to need a chainsaw. Do you want to ride to town with us? It's been a few days since you went to the store."

"Yes," Barbara said, "I appreciate you asking. I do need a few things. I'll grab my purse," she said, as she turned to retrieve it. Clair and Dana walked to the truck. Clair climbed in as Dana waited for Barbara, unsure of where she wanted to sit.

Barbara appeared carrying her purse and walked to the truck. "I'll sit between my two handsome men," she said, as she could see Dana was waiting to get in.

Barbara slid in, taking out a kerchief as she settled and tied it around her long gray hair. Dana slid beside her and shut the door as Clair started the truck. "Come on Duke," he hollered out the window out of habit, but Duke was already at the end of the drive, waiting.

"So Dana," Barbara inquired, "what do you think about the wood processor?"

Dana responded, "I thought it was pretty neat."

She talked about how beautiful a spot it was over there and then asked Clair, with concern on her face, "I hope you warned Dana about the dangers of Granite Hill."

"That's tomorrow," Clair said, sounding a little irritated.

"Well, you make sure you do," she cautioned, "it's a dangerous place on that side of the river."

Dana's interest was piqued. *What could be so dangerous?* he wondered. He sat silently, hoping more would be said, but there wasn't. He would have liked to ask but Clair had sounded grouchy about it. Besides, he thought, Clair said he would tell him about it tomorrow. *If he doesn't, then I'll ask*, Dana decided.

The truck pulled into town and turned right, behind the baseball backstop, along the maple-lined common which was now on their left, in front of the Protestant church with its white steeple, then bearing left, following the circular common. Clair parked in front of Rob's market.

"How long will you be?" Barbara asked Clair as she was sliding across the seat to the door that Dana had opened.

"Oh, if you give us a half hour that would be enough time," Clair answered.

"If I'm not out front I'll be in the post office visiting with Alice, so just pull up there," Barbara said.

The post office was in the same brick block as the store, but on the right side of the building, with the store taking up the rest. Barbara had gone to grade school with Alice and they were childhood friends. Barbara usually would try to visit with her when she came to town. Alice became post mistress during the Second World

War and had kept the job when Mr. Attler, the former post master, didn't return home from the war.

"Ok," Clair said, putting the truck in gear just as Duke caught up. "Just going over to Johnson's," Clair called out his window to Duke, as if he understood what he was saying.

Around the common they drove, past the court house where a few months before Clair showed up just in the nick of time, bearing left past the service station on the corner and continued on past the Masonic temple, where Dana had always heard that important people in town met and performed secret rituals, which nobody who wasn't asked to join knew what they meant. Dana didn't know anyone who was a Mason.

Almost directly across from Rob's market and almost back to where they first turned, the truck stopped in front of Johnson's General Store.

Johnson's was a big wooden building with a covered porch that ran across its wide front. It had three loading docks down its deep left side. The right side had a big mural painted on it of a rainbow trout jumping out of the water to catch an unsuspecting fly. A few years back, a traveling artist looking to make a name for himself spent the summer painting several buildings and barns in the area with different colorful nature scenes. Johnson's, with its big, long, bare wall, was a lucky recipient. The artist didn't charge anyone for his work; he left the area as fall set in and hadn't been seen or heard from since. But the beautiful artwork remained.

There were wooden railings along the front porch that not so many years before people used to tie their horses and wagons to. The porch could be entered from the front center, where a wide set of stairs made of granite lay, or from either end. The cement troughs that use to catch the rain water from the roof and gutters and hold water for the horses tied out front had long been filled with topsoil and now had colorful flowers flowing from them.

Johnson's sold almost everything to help carve out a living in northern Vermont, including most any kind of hardware, animal feed, seed, fertilizer, tools, finished lumber, building supplies, farming machinery, logging equipment, milking supplies, plumbing needs, hunting and fishing supplies and much, much more. Everything, it seemed, except for food. That was for Rob's to sell. It was said that if Johnson's didn't have it or couldn't get it, you didn't need it.

Dana followed Clair up the front granite steps to the double screened doors.

There were two old men dressed in overalls sitting to the right of the door in wicker chairs. Next to them was a long wooden bench made of a half cut pine log turned flat side up. The chairs looked more comfortable, Dana thought. Both acknowledged Clair by name. Clair said hi but didn't call them by name or stop to talk. Getting close to chores, Dana could tell. Dana said hi as he passed and entered the store behind Clair.

It was busy. Unlike the grocery store it was mostly men and very few kids. Everyone was dressed in work clothes, going about their business, gathering off the shelves what they needed, their arms full; there were no shopping carts. Clair walked down through the middle of the store on the old wooden floors, heaved from age in some places, between the shelves piled high with everything imaginable and in no particular order.

He said hi to a few people as he passed but mostly just made his way to the back. He seemed to know where he was going. Dana, walking behind Clair, was amazed how much was in the store and found it near impossible to not stop and look at all what was for sale, but he, like Clair, was on a mission and dutifully followed.

They continued through another set off doors and reached a back counter. The smell of gas and oil was heavy in the air. Almost like being in a garage, Dana thought. Behind the counter was a man with glasses hanging low on his nose, working on some mechanical device that Dana didn't recognize. Dana could see he was deep in thought as he fiddled with the contraption.

His thick hands were creased and dirty with grease. The cigarette hanging from the corner of his mouth looked the same, as it had been handled with the same hands. Dana thought it was funny the man would dare to smoke with the heavy smell of gasoline in the air.

The man looked up when he realized someone was standing there. A quick, easy smile came across his face when he recognized who it was, bellowing, "Well if it isn't Clair Phillips." He set down what he was working on to wipe some of the grease off his hands, and took the grease-stained cigarette from his mouth and set it down too.

He stuck out his hand to shake Clair's and said, "Sorry it took so long to notice you but that carburetor was giving me fits," the man explained. "How the hell are ya?" he asked as he shook Clair's hand.

"I'm good, Charlie," Clair said, shaking his hand in return.

"Great!" said Charlie. "And who's this fella?" Charlie asked, acknowledging Dana.

"This," Clair said, "is Dana Thompson. Dana, this is Charlie Johnson, owner of this place." Clair added, "Dana's been staying with Barbara and I, giving us a hand on the farm."

"Yes, yes, yes!" said Charlie as he shook Dana's hand. "I guess I heard that. Joe Lanou's grandson, right?" he asked Dana, but clearly already knowing the answer.

"Yup," Dana said, proud that the association had been made. The fact that people knew who his grandfather was made Dana feel more confident.

"Boy," Charlie said, turning his attention back to Clair, "you kinda put Robert Marcoux in his place a few months back."

Clair didn't say anything but wouldn't have had time to anyways before Charlie added, "That's good for the son of a bitch! Couldn't have happened to a nicer guy."

Clair gave a polite smile.

"Charlie, what do you have for a chainsaw?" he asked, glad to get on to another subject.

"What are you looking for?" Charlie asked. Years of selling had taught him to ask the questions first.

"Well," Clair answered, "I would like one of those ones that one person could operate, something lighter."

"Well," Charlie answered, "I have them all. Follow me," he said, and started walking, assuming they were both following. He led them to where he had three saws, two of them one-person saws. Clair hefted the smaller one.

Clair asked a few questions about the saw's capability and Charlie gave answers which satisfied him. Within a few minutes, and some minor dickering about the price, the purchase was complete. Clair also got him to throw in some free files for the chain, all the while Charlie was protesting that he wasn't making a dime, as he started to fill out the sales slip.

"Might as well grab your saw," Clair said to Dana.

Dana reached down and picked the saw up. *For a one-person saw it sure is heavy,* he thought, his confidence shaken, and wondered if he would be able to run it.

Clair, sensing Dana's uneasiness, assured him that he would be able to handle it. Dana still wasn't sure, but Clair's words did help.

Charlie finished writing up the slip and turned it around for Clair to sign. "Thank you both," he said, as Clair put down the pen.

Charlie stepped closer to Dana. "Did a lot of business with old Joe," he said softly. "He was a good man," looking Dana in the eye with a serious expression, as though to validate what he said.

"Thanks," Dana said, "I appreciate that." Clair and Dana headed out the way they came in, with Dana carrying the saw.

There seemed to be more people in the store now than when they came in. Dana was sure he was going to catch somebody with the chain before he got out but he made it to the front door without doing any damage.

The two old men were still on the porch when Dana walked out with his saw. "Boy," one said to the other, "they sure don't make those saws like they use to," and they both fell into stories about logging camp and the good old days. Dana could still here them talking even after he put the saw in back of the truck and they were pulling away to go pick up Barbara on the other side of the common.

"Charlie seems like a nice guy," Dana said to Clair.

"He is," Clair agreed, "a little bit of a salesman, but he is a nice guy."

It had been almost a half hour on the nose. Clair pulled up in front of the post office.

Barbara must have been watching; she was walking out the front door as Clair stopped the truck. "Pull over there," Barbara mouthed, motioning towards the store as she walked that way.

Clair backed up and said to Dana, "We must not be the only ones to have bought a lot."

They pulled up in front of the store and before Dana and Clair could get out two young boys immediately came out of the store, one carrying a 100 lb sack of flour and the other a 100 lbs of sugar. They plopped them in the back of the truck and went to grab a couple smaller bags.

Dana opened his door to let Barbara in as she thanked the boys who had carried her groceries.

"I guess you plan to do a little baking," Clair commented to her as she settled in her seat.

"You know I have many to care for," was all she said.

Dana thought the comment a little odd but he was still wondering if he was going to be able to handle the chainsaw. "Besides," Barbara quipped, "by the looks of that saw I think I'm going to have to feed Dana more."

"I think you're right," Dana said.

The Ford truck headed south towards the farm. Clair took the saw and put it in the workshop while Dana unloaded the flour and sugar.

The cows were waiting by the fence gate to be let in the barn and milked. Chores went smoothly and supper followed soon after. Dana took a shower immediately after supper, and after saying goodnight, went to bed. It was still daylight but it had been a long day. A very eventful day, and he was exhausted.

Dana awoke from a deep sleep. He had heard voices again. A lot like the first night he was there when he thought it was a dream. He listened as he put his face close to the alarm clock, straining his eyes to see what time it was. It was ten pm. He had been sleeping a couple of hours.

Was he just dreaming like the first night? he wondered. Dana could see the light was on in the kitchen by the way it shone up through his register.

He could make out Clair's voice. There was Barbara's. But there was a third. He lay still, trying to make out what was being said, but it was muffled.

Dana swung his feet to the floor and crept to the register. It was just so unusual to have someone this late in the house. He looked down through the register to the kitchen but couldn't see anyone. He got down on his hands and knees and peered at an angle towards the strange voice. He could see the stranger. If only he would come one step closer he would be able to see him real good.

He waited, trying to hear what they were saying, but they were still talking too softly.

Wait! The stranger had moved closer to the register. Dana could now see him from the waist down. He had work pants on. What was it he had in his hands? He could almost see! If he would just turn a little....there, now he could see. It looked like two bigger bags tied into a knot up top. One looked to be sugar, the other with flour, he guessed, judging by the looks of the bags he had seen earlier.

Now the man was coming closer so that Dana was going to be able to see his face. Just a little more... There! But the man had a hat on. It blocked his face from above. It was a three-corner hat like the old timers used to wear back in the revolutionary war that Dana had seen in the history books. *Where have I seen this guy before?* If only he could see his face. *Wait,* Dana thought, *I know!*

Suddenly the comment Barbara had made in the truck made more sense. When Clair asked Barbara if she was going to do a lot of baking she had replied that she had many to take care of. This guy standing below him in the kitchen, Dana had seen late one night in Mill village. He recognized the hat.

He had heard a dog barking late one night and seen someone across the street on the neighbor's porch through his bedroom window. He couldn't see him well, but could make out the distinctive hat. He had run downstairs and looked out the living room window and saw him walking away, and clearly saw the hat again when he walked under the dim street light.

Dana had opened the door to get a better look but the guy was gone. He stepped out on the porch and almost tripped over something. It was only when he brought it in did he realize it was food. He told Aunt Polly about it next morning. She wasn't surprised. The food had been there before. Not only at their house but also at several of the neighbors who had kids.

Wow! Dana thought. *Barbara and Clair were the ones responsible. Wow! They were just real super people, people who cared about the less fortunate.*

Dana climbed back into bed after the stranger said goodbye and left through the back kitchen door. He wanted to ask Clair and Barbara about it but didn't want them to think he was snooping. He'd think of a way to ask. Maybe he'd even get the chance to help the stranger pass out the food. That would be way too neat. Dana hoped to get the chance to meet him soon.

Chapter 12

Dana slept fitfully and woke when Clair first stirred downstairs.

He'd had crazy dreams the rest of the night about masses of people needing food. He dreamt he had a truckload full but when the canvas was pulled back, nothing was there but wood. His partner helping him was the stranger from the night before, but as in real life, Dana could never glimpse his face.

He needed to find the right time to ask about last night. He needed to find the right time, or maybe it would come up in conversation at breakfast. He would bide his time.

After chores were finished Dana readied for breakfast. Barbara was in her usual sunny mood as she shuffled back and forth between the stove, refrigerator and table preparing breakfast.

The three sat down to a mountainous pile of pancakes and warmed maple syrup. Dana was eager to dig into Barbara's new butter, made the day before.

"How did you sleep?" Barbara asked Dana as he was slicing into the butter, lifting his pancakes and depositing the contents from the end of his knife between the steaming cakes to melt in.

"Ok," Dana lied, as he complemented the butter by pouring the maple syrup over his stack, watching it drizzle over the sides and collect in the bottom of the plate.

"I had funny dreams," he continued, realizing that this might be the perfect time to bring up the stranger. "I thought I heard voices late," he added, hoping that what he said might spark the conversation he was looking for.

"Well," Barbara said. Dana held his breath, waiting for her to continue. "I guess I had better keep that radio turned down when someone is trying to sleep." Dana smiled in acknowledgement, as his mouth was now filled with pancakes, butter and syrup. She was unwilling to bring it up so he would wait, he decided.

Clair changed the subject when he said, "We're going to let the cows out to pasture tonight for the first time. I hope that there is more room on the milk truck as this is surely going to increase production. When you see the milk man today would you ask him to leave another can?" he asked Barbara, more serious than what Dana had thought at first.

"Why don't we cut them back one bale to five on hay too, Dana. If they're out on grass they won't eat as much hay," Clair directed. "We'll see if they clean that up and we'll adjust it accordingly," he added.

"So," Barbara said, "today is the first day with the chainsaw. I hope you boys are careful. Those things make me so nervous," she continued, making a face that showed her alarm. "You make sure you talk to Dana about the other side of the river too," she scolded Clair. "You promised me you would yesterday on our way to town." She looked at Clair determinedly as she talked.

"I didn't promise you anything, but yes, I will tell him," Clair responded, after a slight hesitation in which Barbara was going to say more, but Clair answered in time.

They were talking as if Dana wasn't there. In a way, he wasn't. He was trying to figure out how he could turn the conversation to the night before. Now Barbara had given him the perfect opportunity to. Dana would wait until Clair brought up the river. *That would be the perfect time,* Dana strategized.

With breakfast finished, Dana excused himself and went to the sink to wash the sticky syrup off his face and hands. He couldn't wait to go to the woods. It was an exciting day. Not only was he going to learn how to run the saw, he was going to be able to use the wood processor again, even learn more about it, as Clair had said when they left yesterday.

But most of all Dana was going to hear what was so dangerous about the other side of the river, and then spring his question about the stranger.

Clair and Dana readied the trailer, including the new saw with a jug of oil and gas and the lunch basket that Barbara had once again filled. The peaveys and small pile of wood were there from the day before. Clair engaged the clutch with Dana sitting next to him and headed for the woods, with Duke trailing behind.

I wonder if he'll keep up today, Dana only half wondered to himself because of the four pancakes Duke wolfed down that were left over from breakfast, fully knowing that it wouldn't slow him one bit.

Dana opened the gates and closed them as he had the day before, with Duke taking the lead soon after they exited the main road. It was another blue sky day with a few more clouds than yesterday, but mostly sunshine nevertheless.

When they reached the canopy of maples, Clair and Dana pointed out to one another their next victims to be sacrificed by way of their new saw. Dana had to agree with his grandfather's assessment that was conveyed through Clair; with a forest this large, there did seem to be plenty of wood to be cut without felling a healthy tree.

As the tractor made its way along the road towards the light of the clearing that would expose the face of Granite Hill, Dana paid less attention to the fallen trees and instead readied his thoughts for what lay ahead. Would it be as spectacular as yesterday, or was it something that once you saw it the first time its powerful visual impact lessened every time thereafter?

It took only a few seconds to find out as the tractor pulled into the clearing and exposed the massive face of pure majestic stone stretching skyward, seemingly as high as the clouds above, with the pounding waterfall of Lords Creek in the foreground spraying up plumes of mist and making one's chest pound as the force of the water rushed over the falls and dived into the rocks and pool below. The near-deafening sound wasn't offensive to the ears, but rather had a calming, almost memorizing effect.

No, Dana thought, *this will never get old.*

He momentarily thought of the workers in Mill village. If this were what they saw every day of their working life as they arrived and left for work, they wouldn't look so tired and downtrodden, going to and fro. This had to be one of the most beautiful spots on earth. What could be so dangerous?

Clair pulled the tractor up next to the processor and slowed to a stop. He was about to instruct Dana in what to do, but Dana was already off the tractor. That's what he liked about this boy. Not only did he learn quickly but he didn't have to be told twice. He was eager too, and curious and polite.

Barbara loved having him in the house, too. Occasionally over the years they had hired men and boys to help on the farm. They had never had any real problems. Some worked better than others, and some habits were harder to tolerate than others, but all in all it went well.

Dana was different. For a kid who had every reason to be bitter, no family to speak of, this kid did all right.

Maybe it was a blessing that what happened, happened at an early age like it did. At least there wasn't the memory that could come late at night, or thoughts of what would be, if things were different. Clair had those still.

What was happening now in this kid's life was real, something that he could grasp hold of, something that, with the help from him and Barbara, Dana could control. There would be no more

Robert Marcoux in his life, or at least no one who could threaten to take what was his.

Clair was worried only that his own health wouldn't keep up with a boy, or young man, of fifteen. It wasn't that his health was bad, though his knee bothered him some. He seemed to get winded quicker than he ever had before, too. He and Barbara had come to realize in the last few years that they needed to limit the amount of heavy work they did. The Rabideau brothers did their haying, and they had hired someone to put their wood up. Now Dana would do that. But still, there was plenty to do on a farm for a man and his wife both nearing seventy.

The boy did his chores well. Clair would teach him how to milk next. That would take some pressure off.

And I'm not dead yet, Clair thought to himself. *You're only as good as what you've accomplished at the end of the day, old boy.*

Now that he had an adopted son to teach, one who needed to cut a lot of wood, he would have to figure a way to work smarter. *But for now we'll make do. We'll get it done,* he thought.

He had heard Dana tell him yesterday, almost under his breath that he wouldn't let him down. *By God, as He is my witness, I won't let him down either,* Clair declared silently.

Dana had everything pulled out of the wagon and had the lunch basket in hand, ready to place it in the shade as he had done yesterday. Clair snapped back to the present, placing the tractor in gear to pull it around to finish their load. He backed it in place. Dana was there to unhitch the trailer.

Clair drove the tractor back up top and shut it off. He dismounted to help Dana load the saw in a way that it wouldn't scrape the cutting chain against any metal part of the tractor, dulling it. Dana wrapped the logging chains around the three-point hitch. They were ready.

It was only a few minutes and Clair had the tractor backed up to some larger damaged limbs. Dana hitched the chains as Clair had taught him. The tractor pulled the limbs with ease, dislodging them as they came crashing to the ground. Clair shut off the tractor and grabbed the saw from its resting place. He showed Dana the on/off switch, the choke and where you added gas and oil to keep the saw chain lubricated.

"I need you to watch me a few times," he said to Dana. "There are some do's and don'ts.

"The first, most important thing to remember is respect," Clair began. "If you do not respect what this saw is capable of doing then you are going to get hurt bad, probably killed," he said matter-of-factly. "This saw can cut this whole forest down with ease." He motioned with his head towards the trees for emphasis. "So what do you think it would do to you," Clair asked, "if it came in contact with your skin?" He looked at Dana, waiting for a reply.

"It would probably cut my leg off or whatever it touched," Dana responded.

"No probably about it," Clair warned again.

"Dana," he continued, with his voice low and as serious as Dana had ever heard him in the short time he known him, "many men have lost their lives running these saws. I do not mean to scare you. I do not want you to be scared. I just want you to be aware and cautious and respect this saw's capability when you operate it. Do you understand, Dana?" Clair looked Dana square in the eye to gauge his reaction.

Dana did understand, and was processing everything Clair had warned before he answered. He didn't feel afraid. He didn't feel as though Clair were talking down to him or doubting his ability. Just the opposite, in fact.

Dana looked at the saw held in the old man's hands and then up at Clair and met his stare. "I do understand," he said, his throat tight and dry. "I'll pay attention and be careful," he continued low and slow as if he was talking to himself as much as he was to Clair. "I can run that saw," he finished with calm confidence.

Clair was satisfied.

"What I want you to notice," Clair began, "is how I will always keep the wood I'm cutting between me and the saw. You'll see what I mean when I start it in just a second. Also, probably the number one rule is never, never, saw above your waist. It's too easy for the saw to kick back and cut your face or arm or whatever it comes in contact with," as he demonstrated what it would look like if the saw kicked back.

Clair set the choke and yanked the pull cord once and then twice. The saw sputtered. On the third pull it started. The sound of the saw reverberated through the forest. Dana was surprised how loud it was. A waft of oily smelling smoke drifted by him as Clair revved the saw's throttle. Strangely, it smelled appealing.

Clair stood on one side of the log and cut a limb, keeping the meaty part of the wood between him and the saw as he had instructed Dana. The chain easily sliced through the wood, spitting out large chunks of sawdust, throwing it behind the saw.

Dana watched as Clair worked his way up the log until it was limbless. Clair shut off the saw. "Loud, isn't it?" he said to Dana, smiling.

"Sure is," Dana agreed, adding, "I like the way it smells." Clair laughed and said, "Well, between the noise and smell, it helps keeps the bugs away. Want to try it?" he asked, motioning with a nod towards the saw.

"Yup," Dana said, his typical confident answer.

"I'll have you square up the end here," Clair pointed at the end of the large limb where it was jagged. "That happens to the tree when the limb breaks for whatever reason, whether it's caused by the wind or lightning. It's nice to have it squared so the piston will be able to push it on the processor towards the saw."

Dana picked up the saw. It felt heavy.

"After you start it," Clair instructed, "cut about right here," he pointed to the spot on the log again, "and just let the weight of the saw cut the wood. It will cut almost by itself," he explained. "Whatever you do, though," he warned, "is when it's just about through the log, don't let the saw chain get into the dirt. That will dull your chain and make it a lot harder for the saw to cut."

Dana looked at Clair. Clair nodded towards the saw and then the log. Dana pulled the cord and the saw barked to life. Dana revved and then let off the throttle a couple times and could feel the power of the machine he held in his hands. He positioned the saw on the log and squeezed the throttle. The saw sliced down through the log as easy as his knife did this morning at breakfast in Barbara's new butter.

Man, Dana thought, *this is one powerful tool.*

It was intoxicating to feel the vibration and power. Dana held firmly to the handle as the saw blade finished through the log, careful not to drop the chain into the dirt. Dana stood up with the saw running and faced Clair. Clair made the motion to shut off the saw.

"How was that?" Clair asked as soon as the noise finished echoing out through the trees.

"Great!" Dana responded with a grin ear to ear. "That is neat."

"Well for now we'll concentrate on this smaller stuff," Clair said, referring to the limbs and tree trunks that had broken off. "Soon we'll start to cut some of the dying trees to make room for the young ones," he added. "That will be a whole other lesson. Let's grab a few more and with what you have from yesterday, you can start splitting and I should be able to keep you supplied," Clair challenged.

An hour later they were back at the processor with enough lumber dragged for Dana to start.

"Here," Clair said, as he handed one of the peaveys to Dana. "I know I kind of showed you yesterday but it's better when you have a log."

Clair drove the pointed end into the wood. The clamp-like hook wrapped around the log, enabling Clair to easily roll the log toward the forks of the processor. Dana tried it, clumsily at first but after a couple tries, he too rolled the log with ease.

"Boy," Dana said to Clair, "I can see why you waited until today to try and move these. These peaveys make it a lot easier to move the wood."

"Sure do," Clair acknowledged.

"Let's get this machine uncovered," Clair said, "so I can show you a couple things. You need to get some splitting done. Barbara won't put up with us not bringing home a load today," Clair said, laughing.

Dana laughed and replied, "I would expect our lunches would be getting smaller if we don't."

Clair laughed again and agreed.

Clair showed Dana how to check the fluids on the splitter and explained what each did and at what level they needed to be maintained.

He also showed Dana where the grease fittings were and demonstrated how to use the grease gun for the moving parts of the splitter, ensuring less wear. He also stressed that this was to be the process followed each day before the machine was started. "Ok," Clair announced, "you ready to get this show on the road?" he directed at Dana.

"Yup, sure am." Dana replied.

"Listen," Clair said, looking at Dana with a cautioning tone, "we don't need to bull and jamb. That's how accidents happen and things get broke. Just go at a pace that is comfortable. In a couple hours we'll stop for lunch and see where we're at. Ok?"

Dana gave his customary "Yup."

Clair headed for the tractor. Dana turned on the splitter. The show was on the road.

Dana worked on the pile of seven or so logs. He was amazed how time flew. It seemed like only a few minutes and Clair was back with a few more logs and just a little while later back with some more.

Clair was right, Dana thought as he unhitched the chains so Clair wouldn't have to get off the tractor, *he can keep up with what I can split. That old man is a worker.* He shook his head in amazement. Clair made the finger across the neck motion and pointed to the basket.

Lunch! Dana said to himself.

I wonder what Barbara has made today, as he made his way to the basket and then to the river where Clair was already at the make-shift stone table. Dana wondered if Clair would warn him about the dangers that so concerned Barbara. He hoped so, and then maybe he could ask, depending on Clair's demeanor, about the stranger.

The spot where they ate lunch was at the lower end of the large pool. It was cool with the water flowing past, and far enough below the falls, probably a good hundred yards or so, that one didn't have to holler to carry on a conversation. It was neat to watch the water cascading over the falls from that angle.

Clair dug into the basket. "Ham," he announced happily, as he held out a sandwich to Dana. "Looks like some brownies, too, I'm guessing because she has a jug of milk in here with the tea," he said gleefully, digging further to verify. "Yup," was the pronouncement as he found the brownies after grabbing a sandwich for himself.

Dana finished his first sandwich and stood up to grab another.

"Want some tea?" he offered to Clair as he poured some for himself.

"Please," replied Clair.

Dana caught something out of the corner of his eye at the top of the falls. He jerked his head quickly. It was Duke. He was walking almost as if he was on top of the water from the far side toward the road that brought them to the clearing along the very edge of the falls.

Dana caught himself saying, "How the hell......!" and stopped, not really knowing whether he had swore or not. He was expecting at any moment for Duke to come tumbling over the edge, but he didn't.

That's just not possible, he thought, and looked at Clair in amazement for an explanation. Clair looked up at the falls about the same time that Duke made it to dry ground and was coming towards them with his tongue hanging out and tail wagging.

"Get ready to share a little bit of your lunch," Clair said, breaking the silence, tearing a corner of his sandwich off for the dog. Clair flipped the end to Duke, who caught it and gobbled it in one motion.

Dana looked at Duke, back again at the falls and then to Clair, knowing full well what he saw but not understanding. Clair started talking without acknowledging Dana's bewilderment.

"Have you ever heard people talk about the smuggling days?" Clair asked Dana, as he worked on his second sandwich.

"Yeah," Dana answered, still standing with the tea in his hand, having not yet poured Clair's.

"What have you heard?" Clair asked Dana.

"Well," Dana started, pausing, searching back through his mind to the rumors and myths of his growing up that were told to him by his school mates and others. “I guess,” he continued after he got straight what he remembered, “that the smugglers used to use this river to smuggle stuff; stuff that was illegal, like booze...” Dana said, unsure of what he was supposed to say without sounding like he knew for sure, which he didn’t.

Clair waited before speaking to see if Dana was going to say more. When he knew Dana wasn’t, he spoke again.

“And do you think what you were told was true?” he asked Dana.

Dana was fumbling with the cups to pour Clair’s tea, as he thought about the question Clair asked.

“Well, um... I guess that maybe, um well I guess, I don’t know for sure,” was all that Dana was able to say.

“So what do you think?” Clair continued, not willing to let Dana off the hook that easy.

“Well,” Dana continued again, “I suppose it’s true. I mean why would people say it if it wasn’t?” Dana asked, trying to put the ball back in Clair’s court.

“People say many things that aren’t true,” Clair countered and stopped.

After a couple seconds of silence Dana heard himself asking Clair, “Is it true, were there really smugglers?” He waited, holding his breath, not sure if he was asking something he shouldn’t. It was quiet, even the waterfall seemed silent now as he waited for Clair to answer.

“Yes,” Clair answered, looking up at Dana, “there were.”

Dana let out his breath and took another. “Here?” Dana asked softly, as if any smugglers who might be hiding behind a tree would hear him ask.

"Right here," Clair answered, "right where you're standing."

Dana caught himself looking down at his feet but quickly realized Clair was talking about the river and the falls and looked that way to survey the area where they might have been. He momentarily pictured hooded men, clandestinely sneaking up the river, looking around to who might be watching. He could almost feel himself squatting down so as not to be seen.

Clair spoke again, startling Dana. "They used to come up the river in the middle of the night, and when they made it to the falls they would unload their cargo and hide it up in those ledges," Clair said, pointing to the cliffs of Granite hill.

"Sometime later, when they thought the coast was clear, they would bring wagons and load what they had stored to distribute, or to carry further on to wherever the cargo was intended to go. They laid flat rocks just below the surface of the water on top of the falls, and as long as it wasn't spring time when the water was too high, they could walk across the top of the falls undetected, barely getting their feet wet...like you just saw ole' Duke do," Clair said.

Dana was dumbfounded. He couldn't fully comprehend the story. Right here, Clair had said. Right here on his grandfather's, no, *his* farm. "Does it still happen?" Dana asked.

"Don't think so," Clair said. "It stopped a few years after the war, after they stopped the rationing."

Dana was still just blown away. His mind raced with a thousand questions but he didn't know which ones he should ask. Finally he settled on one.

"Did you know 'em?" Dana asked Clair.

"Know who?" responded Clair, as he was digging through the basket looking for the brownies.

"The smugglers," Dana answered, "did you know the smugglers?"

Clair dumped the tea out of his cup to make way for the milk he was going to dunk his brownie in. He filled his cup to the brim and handed the milk to Dana. "Yeah," he replied, "I knew them."

Dana wanted to ask more but recognized when Clair was done talking about something.

Clair dunked his brownie deep in his milk, letting the frothy white liquid run down his cup. He stuffed better than half of the dessert in his mouth and took a swig to help wash it down. Watching him chew, Dana could see Clair thinking.

Maybe, Dana thought, Clair was thinking about those bad men, those smugglers.

Clair finished his brownie and grabbed another. "Dana," he said, "you heard Barbara ask if I told you about the other side of the river, right?"

"Yes, I did," Dana replied, glad that the conversation had gotten to this point.

"Well, what she is so concerned about," Clair started then corrected himself, starting again, "what *we're* concerned about is that the smugglers didn't want anybody to find their stuff, so they would booby-trap it. Do you know what that means?" Clair asked.

Dana thought and realized he didn't and answered, "No."

"Well," Clair said, "what they would do is set traps that would injure or maim someone if they stumbled upon their stash. Even though the smugglers are gone, I don't want you over there. Am I clear?"

"Yes, you are." Dana replied. And he was. That was, of the few things Clair had cautioned him about, the sternest warning to date, even more than the chainsaw.

Lunch was over. Dana wanted in the worst way to ask him about the stranger last night. It would have to wait. He would try again tomorrow, or when a better time arose.

Dana packed up the basket as Clair walked towards the trailer and the pile of split wood.

Smugglers, he thought, *right where I'm standing. You know, maybe the stranger was a smuggler. Maybe that was why Clair and Barbara kept it a secret. Maybe he was a smuggler tuned nice. Somebody who wanted to do good.*

Dana put the basket next to the splitter. It didn't have to be in the shade now, empty as it was.

"Let's put a couple more hours in," Clair said. "That should give us a load and make mother happy." Clair started the tractor and headed back towards the woods.

Dana was standing by the start switch to the processor. Duke followed behind the tractor. The tractor turned left and disappeared into the woods. Duke turned right and danced across the falls.

Dana heard himself laughing out loud over the sound of the proccssor. *Better you than me, ole' Dukie boy, better you than me.*

CHAPTER 13

Farming is a great life, Dana decided one morning as he was getting ready to head for the woods. As routine as farming was, it was always different, and the people Dana met made it interesting.

Routine in the fact that the cows were milked every twelve hours and there were things that were done on a schedule. The mail man Ken Dean delivered mail six days a week. The milk man came to pick up the milk cans full of milk every day, and there were others who came by too to conduct their business.

Every Wednesday the Purina grain salesman, Steve Palin, would come to take the week's order for a Friday delivery.

Every Tuesday, providing there was a grain bag tied to the mail box signifying that a cow had given birth, or "freshened", as the farmers said, the cattleman Booze Crandall would stop to pick up any bull calves born that week to transport to the live stock commission sales held every Tuesday night.

Sometimes these visitors would have stories or gossip to tell.

Booze Crandall, whose nickname was given to him for his ability or love of drinking, as one would surmise, had a nose that was bigger than average size. It was also unusually red and pock- marked from the effects of alcohol.

From time to time Booze would get picked up by the Sheriff or the State police for weaving when he should have been wagging, and he would lose his license for a while. Booze would have to hire a driver until the time determined by the Judge was served or the fine paid, or both.

The driver was usually a man named Joe, who everybody called Frenchie. He too was as apt to be under suspension at any time for drinking, but when he was able, and Booze needed him, would fill in for Booze.

Frenchie was a likable fellow. He was a man of slight build who looked older than he was. The effects of heavy drinking, smoking and late night card playing, combined with years of occasional physical labor needed to survive in northern Vermont, could do that to a person.

"Where's Booze?" Dana asked Frenchie, as Booze's familiar cattle truck pulled up to the milk house door one morning as Dana was washing the milking equipment after chores.

"Oh, you know," Frenchie started, "Booze has a bit of a problem with the bottle from time to time. Sheriff asked him to take a little break," he continued, as if it had never happened to him.

"Got picked up the other night, late," Frenchie said with emphasis, enjoying being able to tell the story to someone, even though it certainly wasn't the first time that morning he had told it, and certainly wouldn't be the last.

"Where'd he get picked up?" Dana asked, curious himself.

"Well," Frenchie started, "we had just left the poker game after the sale last Tuesday and I told Booze he had too much to drink," Frenchie said, "but he wouldn't listen, and sure enough the Sheriff picked him up," he said with vindication. "Booze forgot to turn his lights on going through town. Sheriff got him not even halfway down Main Street," he said excitedly in his high- pitched voice. "Hauled him right to jail."

"Well that's too bad." Dana said, getting a chuckle out of the high strung French man telling the story, but also feeling bad for Booze's bad luck.

"Sure is," Frenchie said, "but you know, Booze doesn't always make the right decisions." He was obviously hoping that Dana would ask why.

Dana didn't disappoint. "Why's that?" he asked.

"Well, a while back Booze and another one of his cattle dealing friends got to messin' around with a calf over in West Glen," Frenchie said, his voice lower, looking around as he didn't want to be overheard.

"What do you mean by messing around?" Dana asked, curious, thinking that he knew what Frenchie was trying to say but wanting to be sure, and enjoying the little man's story.

"You know," Frenchie said, looking at Dana nodding his head, his chin upwards and eyes wide, "they were pestering her," the man whispered.

"No!" Dana said, "really?" not believing for one second what the slight man was saying, but with too much of the story told, there had to be an ending.

"So what happened?" Dana prodded.

"Well," Frenchie said, his voice squeaking with excitement, "I told them to stop, told them it wasn't right. They wouldn't listen. Kept right at it. Booze's friend would hold the wheel barrow so Booze could do the pestering and wouldn't you know it, it happened!"

Dana waited, but Frenchie was done. "What happened?" Dana asked, when he knew that Frenchie wasn't going to tell any more.

"They got that that heifer pregnant!" Frenchie said, his high-pitched voice at a feverish squeal.

Dana burst out laughing, "That's just not possible," Dana said, trying to explain to Frenchie but realizing it wouldn't matter.

"That's what I thought, too," Frenchie exclaimed "until I saw it myself."

"Really?" Dana said, his curiosity getting the best of him. "What did you see?

"Well, you know that museum over there in West Glen, just behind the library?" Frenchie asked, his eyes wide, talking so fast he was spitting. He was referring to a town twenty miles to the west.

"No," Dana said, "I didn't know they had one there."

"Well they do, and in it they have a stuffed calf," Frenchie exclaimed, "and do you know how I know he's the father?" he asked, referring to Booze. His arms were waving in every direction, almost jumping out of his boots.

"No," Dana said, "how do you know?" just not believing what this little man was telling but excited to hear the end of the story.

"Well," Frenchie announced, "because that calf has a nose just like Booze Crandall's!"

Chapter 14

It was July in Vermont. For the Phillips farm that meant it was time to hay. The Rabideau brothers were done their first cut, and as they waited for their second cut to grow, they were ready to put in Clair's hay, as they had done for the last few years.

The Rabideaus had finished Dana's farm the week before and even offered to pay some money for the hay. Dana talked it over with Clair, and the two decided that because the brothers had always taken care of the land, including spreading manure on it and keeping the edges pushed back, that no money would change hands.

Clair's farm had seventy-five acres of hay fields, totaling nine thousand bales, give or take a couple hundred. The Rabideaus were of the new age: Cut your hay early and you could cut it again a second time. Some of the more advanced farmers even tried for three. Clair was happy with one. Besides, one cut was all the barn could hold. The cows could pasture the second cut. By that time their pastures had run down and the new grass gave them a boost. A couple weeks and it would be all done, providing the weather cooperated.

Dana was doing well with the wood. With Clair's help he was splitting and bringing home a cord a day. Six cord a week because Sunday was a day to rest, unless, of course, there was hay down.

Clair had taught Dana how to milk, which gave Clair time to go to the woods early to pull some logs for Dana. It was easier on his knee, he had told Dana.

That old man is amazing, Dana would think every time he would see the pile of wood the old man would have ready for him, although he doubted it was any easier on him. But the old man was going to do what he wanted to do. That was the old stubborn, Yankee way and it wasn't about to change any time soon.

The deal that Clair and the Rabideaus had made was simple: Clair would mow the hay with his cycle bar and then condition it, running it through some rubber rollers to crush the stems to help in the drying process. The Rabideaus would use a tedder to spread the hay out so that it would dry, rake it into windrows when it was dry, and then bale it.

The Rabideaus would then pile the hay onto wagons and bring it to the barn to be stored. They would use a hay elevator to reach the highest parts of the barn, stacking the hay to the highest peaks.

Clair and the boys had an arrangement about money, so much per bale.

First things first, however. What little hay left over from the previous year was stacked over the heifer barn to be fed to the young stock; the milk cows always got the best and freshest.

Clair wasn't going to be able to drag logs for a few weeks, so that meant Dana would be left alone. Dana would help when the hay was baled and ready to be picked up and stored, but in the meantime, the wood business was all his.

Since Clair had given him tractor driving lessons and he had used the chainsaw some, this was a big step in manhood. He was going to turn 16 in a month or so and Clair was confident that Dana would be fine on his own. Barbara was nervous; she had lived it before. It wasn't anything new. Boys became young men, little girls became young ladies and life went on. The sun shone, the hay grew and soon another season came and went.

Barbara had become attached to this boy. His politeness, his gentleness was so out of character for a youth of his age. He had an easy laugh that went with a broad smile; a handsome boy, too, with his dirty blond hair flowing from underneath his cap. It seemed as he had grown a foot taller since he had arrived, but certainly the hard work and good food had filled his lanky frame.

This boy had been good for Clair too. Barbara could feel herself getting older. The cold seemed to linger longer in her bones, the summers shorter. But Clair was the one who seemed to slow. He wouldn't admit it, the stubborn old fool, and she worried for him. She had noticed his shortness of breath. He took rest where he never had before.

She could tell he had become attached to the boy as well. He showed more patience with Dana than any of the others. Clair had even taught him how to milk. How the old girls in the barn must have thought that strange. For years, the only one to have milked them was Clair.

Barbara felt her thoughts drifting back. The emotion still strong; a mother's love. How might things have been different had their little boy lived? He would have been almost forty-five now. Would he have still have been here on the farm, most certainly he would have had a family, maybe there would have been grandkids.

Don't go there, she told herself. There is nothing that could have been done different. He was born a couple months early and everybody did all that could be done, she told herself again. It's just what happened. It was the happiest and saddest week of her life.

For Clair too, although he never talked about it. She had seen him, during that week, not every year but at times, looking up at the hill. That big granite face where their son was buried. She would feel his heavy arm reach for her in the night as they lay in bed and hear his heavy sigh. And they would hug.

Clair wouldn't let anything happen to this boy. If he allowed him to go to the woods alone then Clair must think him ready. Not to worry, she said to herself. But she still would.

CHAPTER 15

Dana checked with Clair one last time before he headed for the woods.

"What time do you think the Rabideau boys will be ready to bale?" he asked Clair.

Clair, bent over the cycle bar mower with the grease gun attached to one of the fittings, stood up and looked at the sky with a trained eye. He scanned the horizon and bent back over the mower and gave a few pumps on the grease gun until the grease squirted out of the fitting.

"I think you had better plan on being back here by one," Clair answered, after processing what his glance towards the sky had told him. "That will give you time to have a little lunch before they start baling," as he gave another pump on the gun.

"You're just going to pull some logs today, aren't you?" It was more of a statement than a question.

"Yup," Dana answered over his shoulder, walking towards the John Deere, eager to get started.

"Don't get cocky with that saw," Clair warned him, as he wiped the excess grease away from the end of the gun with a rag he had pulled from his pocket, now that he was finished greasing the mower.

"I'll be careful," Dana assured him.

He started the tractor and looked around for Duke. Dana eased the hand clutch forward and gave a little throttle. The tractor jerked forward. *Not quite as smooth as Clair,* he thought, *but at least I didn't stall it,* which made him thankful.

"Come on, Duke," he hollered, but Duke was already at the end of the drive, waiting.

Clair watched the tractor roll down the drive. He winced as Dana ground the gears as he up shifted to a higher one. *Getting better,* Clair thought, *but he still needs a little work,* grading Dana's shifting performance.

Dana liked driving the tractor. It was surely something he would boast to his friends in school about. Although a lot of them lived on, and many worked on farms in the summer, he doubted many of them had ever driven one. And with certainty he knew that very few had ever run a chain saw. He would have a lot to tell about.

Dana turned down the lane that divided Clair's farm from his and stopped at the gate.

He still caught himself calling it his grandfather's farm when he talked out loud. It was just hard to comprehend at times. Growing up it was always his grandfather's farm, as if one day he would rise from the ashes of the old homestead to assume ownership. Dana knew that wouldn't happen. He was the Steward of the land now. Just the awesomeness of that thought still caught him off guard at times, though it was starting to sink in.

Dana hopped off the tractor to open the gate. He hopped back down to close it after driving through. *I don't know why we open and then close them when we're going to come back through in a few hours,* he thought, *but Clair says you never leave a gate open. I'll have to ask him why next time I'm with him.*

Because Dana was only going to drag logs to the splitter he hadn't brought the trailer.

Clair and he had found an area of the woods earlier that summer that needed to be thinned out. It was mostly white and yellow birch with a little ash mixed in and their canopies had grown so that it was blocking the sun, not allowing the young maples to grow.

Driving carefully through the woods, along a makeshift woods road the two had cleared, Dana saw a big stump of a tree that Clair and he had cut a few weeks before.

It was the remnant of a huge white birch Clair had shown Dana. Clair explained to Dana how the Indians would strip huge pieces of bark from the trunk of these trees to make their canoes, using pine pitch to help seal the canoes and keep them water-tight. Dana had read about that in school, but it sure was a lot more fun to see it in person.

After Clair had stripped several big pieces of bark from the tree, he further explained to Dana how the Indians and early settlers would use the birch bark to start a fire. Before Dana knew what was happening, Clair had pulled out some matches from the front pocket of his overalls.

"Watch this," he had said.

Dana watched Clair light some of the bark hanging from the tree. Slowly at first, the fire caught, dancing up the hanging bark, shooting up little black puffs of smoke. The fire worked up several inches and then a foot higher until it caught more loose bark. And then more and more and more. Dana watched in amazement, nervous at first as the fire raced up the trunk towards the upper limbs stretched to the sky. It seemed that the whole tree was now ablaze, sending black smoke billowing into the air. The sounds of the crackling bark seemed to echo through the whole forest. After a couple minutes, almost as quick as it started, the fire was done.

"It only burns the loose bark," Clair explained. "Once it gets to the trunk and green stuff it goes out. What'd you think of that?" he had asked him with a boyish grin on his face.

Dana remembered answering, "That is neat," and then asking, "But does it hurt the tree?"

"Well, it probably isn't the best thing that could happen to it," Clair had admitted. "The only reason I would do it is because we're going to cut it down anyways."

Dana stopped the tractor close to a couple smaller trees that were clumped together. They were close to eighteen inches on the stump. Clair had warned him before to only cut the smaller ones when he was by himself. These two would do.

Dana picked up the chainsaw from its resting spot behind the tractor and walked over to the first tree. He looked up at the higher branches to see if there was any wind, and if there was, from which direction it was coming from. Clair had told him that even the best lumberjack would have a hard time making a tree fall against the wind. Dana then noted, after determining there was no wind, which way the tree was leaning. He walked around the tree and picked the place he would notch it. That would determine where the tree fell.

Dana set the choke on the saw. Three pulls of the cord and it roared to life.

He turned the saw on its side and aimed the chain at the tree, working the throttle at the same time. The chain easily bit into the tree, spitting out huge chunks of sawdust. Dana stopped when he was a third of the way through the tree and pulled his saw out. He angled the chain above his first cut and worked the throttle again, cutting at an angle into the tree to complete his notch.

Dana walked around the tree and took one last look above to make sure the wind hadn't picked up. He turned the saw on its side and, cutting from the back of the tree, worked the blade towards his first cut. The tree began to shudder. Just before the saw made it all the way through, the tree leaned towards the notch Dana had made and started to fall in that direction. Dana pulled the blade out and stepped back a few feet. The tree crashed to the ground right where Dana had intended it to fall. *Clair would be proud,* Dana thought.

Dana walked down the length of the tree, cutting off the limbs. He cut the bigger limbs up into small lengths, no more than fourteen inches, and threw them in a pile. Kitchen wood, Clair called it. Good for the kitchen woodstove.

Dana cut down the second tree and had the same success. He backed the tractor around and got the chains hitched around his logs.

There, Dana thought, as he started with his logs towards the splitter. *That went well.*

When Dana got to the clearing he stopped for a moment to take in the view. *This will never get old. They shouldn't even call this work.*

Dana pulled the logs to the processor and unhitched them. He looked over at the long pool of water below the falls where Clair and he would always have their lunch.

You know, as hot as it is right now, if I finish up early I think I'm going for a swim.

Dana pointed the tractor towards the woods, checking his watch. The last hitch had taken a little over an hour. It was ten past eleven right now. If the second hitch took about the same amount of time, that would work. It was twelve fifteen when Dana unhitched his second load. He was drenched in sweat. Not only had it gotten considerably warmer, but he had convinced himself, no matter what, he was going to get his swim in, so he had pushed himself.

Dana stepped down to the water's edge to the lunch rock, as Clair and he called it. He unlaced both his boots and pulled them off. He then pulled off his socks and stuffed them in his boot.

He pulled up his pant legs and stepped towards the water. *Might as well see how warm it is. Brrr! Not warm at all!* He shivered as he put one foot in and then the other. *In fact, it's downright cold!*

Dana contemplated not going in. *Chicken,* he thought, *you worked yourself all up, in fact worked double time so that you would have time, and now you're not going in?* Dana wiggled his toes in the cool water. It didn't feel as cold as when he first stepped in. *The heck with it.*

Dana pulled his shirt over his head and undid his belt to pull his pants off, looking around to make sure nobody had all of a sudden appeared. He laid his pants on the lunch rock where he had draped his shirt. *Better take my watch off too,* he remembered.

Dana stood there with just his underwear on. *Aw the heck with it,* he decided, and pulled them off too.

Standing in the water up to his knees, Dana reached down to scoop some water up to splash on his naked body. *Boy, it is cold.* He looked down at his manhood. "You sure got small in a hurry," he chuckled to himself.

"Ok, on the count of three you're diving in," he said, trying to psych himself up. "One, two, three!" Dana launched his body towards the middle of the pool, disappearing under the cool mountain water and surfacing halfway between the end of the pool and the falls.

Treading water and catching his breath, he fought against the current trying to push him downstream. Dana couldn't remember ever feeling this alive. He turned to look at the falls. On the right hand side there were some rocks that it looked like he could climb up on. Dana swam against the current, working himself that way.

He got off to one side where the swimming was easier. Reaching the outcrop of rocks, he pulled himself up. They were smooth, rounded and slippery. Careful not to jam his foot and toes, Dana stood and faced the falls. The roar of the water was deafening from here. The spray from the plummeting water almost made him invisible at times. Dana could feel the power of the water surging through his body. At that moment he felt invincible.

Dana looked up through the spray to the top of the falls, twelve feet up. *Just too cool,* he thought.

The water was really moving as a leaf came rushing over the falls, disappearing in the water and spray, reappearing a few seconds later halfway way down the pool.

There's got to be fish in here, Dana thought. *I wonder, if I dove in, could I see them?*

Dana steadied himself, took a deep breath and dove away from the falls. The cold, refreshing water enveloped his body as he swam underwater downstream. He could see nothing but rushing, white water at first. As the current pushed him further downstream, his vision cleared. It surprised him how well he could now see.

Turning towards the falls, and fighting the current, Dana saw it. It wasn't the thirty or so small trout that got him excited. It was the big monster that he saw. By far the biggest fish in real life that he had ever seen. It was the granddaddy of them all. It had to be two feet long!

Dana rose to the surface to catch his breath. Treading water, he took several deep gasps of air. On the third one he dove back under. There it was again, just a huge fish! It didn't have a care in the world as the smaller ones kept their distance.

Dana held his breath as long as he could, watching the big lunker. *It has to be a rainbow,* he thought. When he could hold his breath no longer he rose to the surface.

He let the current push him downstream and swam to the side when he was even with his clothes. Dana leaned against the lunch rock to catch his breath. *That is one big fish,* he said to himself, *and I'm going to catch him,* he vowed.

He stood in the sun, still naked, letting nature dry him off. Standing there thinking about the fish he suddenly felt like he was being watched.

He jerked his head toward the processor as he reached for his clothes. Seeing no one, he scanned the other side of the river, and then downstream; still no one. He looked to the top of the falls. Just appearing from the ledges, preparing to cross the top of the falls, was Duke. "Oh, it's just you, Duke," Dana said out loud. "I guess I'm safe," he chuckled to himself.

CHAPTER 16

Summer evenings in Vermont are what front porches were made for.

After chores were finished, supper done and the dishes washed and put away, but still too early for dessert, there was still plenty of daylight left.

Unlike winter, where at four-thirty in the afternoon darkness settles fast, summer seems to take its time, as if Mother Nature has too much beauty to show in one day before she turns out the lights. It could be well after nine pm if the sky was clear before the birds stopped chirping and the meadow peepers started peeping, signifying nighttime.

Sitting on the porch, watching the sunlight slowly fade behind the western mountain range, being chased ever so slightly by the cool, gentle breezes of early evening, one could get a sense of the beauty of Vermont's highest rugged peaks as they were silhouetted against the twilight sky.

Looking north, one could watch the lights of the white steeple of the Protestant church nearly two miles away flicker to life.

Just waving to the vehicles that traveled north and south, knowing who most of them were, and probably where they were going, was relaxing, and a great way to end a busy day. Occasionally one of the vehicles would stop and the person or occupants would climb up the stairs to set and visit. Stories would be told of present and past or just about what was going on around.

One early Friday evening, before dessert, Maurice Lafoe pulled up the drive. A construction worker by trade, it wasn't uncommon for him to be just getting into town after working away all week.

"Hi, Maurice," Clair hollered out with a wave, before the car had even stopped. "What you been up to?" he asked, as he motioned him to the porch. Maurice climbed out of the car with a brown paper bag in one hand that was crumpled up near the top, and a bottle of beer in the other.

"Hey, folks," he returned, acknowledging Barbara and Dana as he shook Clair's hand.

"Beer?" he asked Clair, holding out the crumpled bag.

"No thanks," Clair said, adding, "just had supper."

"Do you know Dana?" Clair asked him, nodding in Dana's direction.

"Nope, but I heard he was staying with you folks," Maurice answered, looking at Dana and giving him a nod.

"I worked for his grandfather some when I was growing up, though," Maurice said to Clair.

"In fact, he gave me my first paying job," nodding to Dana again as he continued talking to Clair.

"I didn't know that," Clair replied, surprised. "Doing what?" Dana sat up in his chair, paying closer attention to the visitor.

"Well," Maurice answered, "we stacked wood, or should I say, I stacked a lot of wood as Joe threw it down cellar," he added, spreading his arms apart for emphasis, looking at Dana, as he had noticed Dana's reaction when he had mentioned his grandfather.

"Joe had a big pile thrown near the cellar window, ready to be put downstairs," Maurice said, pausing to take a long swill of his beer. "I don't know if you remember or not, but you could just barely stand up down there," Maurice said, looking at Clair, pausing to let him acknowledge his question before continuing.

"No," Clair said, "I guess I don't remember his cellar."

"Of course I was young and not so tall," Maurice continued, "but even then I spent most of the day hunched over, lugging and piling the wood as Joe threw it in the window," he said with a pained look on his face. "We only stopped for lunch." He took another long drink, finishing the beer, and reached for another. "But we got it done," he said triumphantly.

"So I climbed back out the window," he continued, after popping the top off his fresh beer, "and Ole' Joe asked me, 'So how much do I owe ya?'

"Well, as I told you, it was my first paying job and I had no idea what to say or even charge," Maurice said, his voice rising for effect as any good storyteller does as the story was reaching its climax.

"So finally Joe says, 'I'll tell ya what, I'm going to pay you three dollars,'" Maurice said, his voice louder than ever. "I couldn't believe it," he exclaimed, "and just as I was about ready to fall over dead thinking he was really going to pay me three whole dollars, ole' Joe said, 'But I'm going to take back two dollars for teaching you how to do it!'"

Maurice erupted into laughter, slapping his knee with his free hand, looking around to see if everybody else was laughing too; they were.

As Dana laughed at the story, he tried to envision where in the burned-out cellar hole the window would have been.

Dana liked the story. It gave new life to his grandfather. Even though he had never seen a picture of him, Dana could see him.

All the other stories he had heard contained no humor, just seriousness. Barbara got up and excused herself.

"Could I get you some dessert?" she asked the visitor.

"Oh, no thanks," Maurice answered, "I've got to get going. I've been away all week."

"How's your father-in law-doing?" Clair asked Maurice as Barbara disappeared inside.

Maurice's father-in-law Jack Farley and he had grown up together. He was quite a fellow who, on a whim or a moment's notice, would up and sell just about everything he had. Usually drinking was the cause of it. Two months later or so he would start all over again. However unconventional it seemed, he always seemed to come out on top.

"Oh pretty good I guess," Maurice said, adding, "I haven't heard that he sold out this week!" causing both he and Clair to laugh.

"Did I ever tell you the time I came home from the service on leave?" Maurice asked.

"Nope, I don't think you did," Clair answered, fully knowing another story was coming.

"Well, it was the middle of February and boy was it cold," Maurice started. "I ended up walking the last five miles to his house, just about froze to death."

Maurice grabbed the last beer out of crumpled paper bag, set his empties back in the bag, and continued.

"It was about ten pm and Jack and Harriet were still up," Maurice said, now starting to slur his words. "Jack was doing some book work at the kitchen table and Harriet was in the parlor doing something, I'm not sure what. Jack was happier than hell to see me and even happier when I pulled out a fifth of whiskey from underneath my coat."

Maurice was right into storytelling now and hardly paused.

"Well you know what Harriet thinks of me anyways, and you know especially how she feels about drinking," he said. Clair had just barely enough time to acknowledge Maurice's half questions before he started again.

"Well, I asked Jack after we said hello and all if he would like a drink. Of course you know what he said," Maurice paused, as he picked up his bottle and guzzled better than half of it in one swig.

"I've never known him to say no," Clair said, letting Maurice continue.

"Well he kind of yells to Harriet in the next room to get the honey and sugar out. That's how he likes to drink his whisky when it's cold outside, mixed with some hot water," Maurice explained as if Clair didn't know.

"Yup, I know that's how he likes it," Clair said.

"As you can imagine, Harriet wasn't too happy but she got out her stool so she could reach the honey and sugar on top of the hutch."

"She doesn't like drinking much," Clair said.

Maurice barely let the words get out of Clair's mouth before he continued.

"So she mixed us up both a drink and set them down in front of us. She says to Jack, 'You're only having one,'" Maurice mimicked his mother-in-law's voice. "So she turns around to put the sugar and honey away and what does Jack do? He grabs the bottle of whisky off the table when her back is turned and starts chugging it as fast as he can," Maurice said, pretending he has the bottle of whisky, chugging it like Jack did.

"And just as she turns around," Maurice said excitedly, "he sets it down like nothing happened. So we finish that drink and Jack hollers in to the room, 'Harriet, Maurice and I will have one more!' So you know what kind of response that brings," Maurice said.

"I can only imagine," Clair responded.

"Well out she comes in to the kitchen just a fuming and grabs her stool. Just as soon as her back is turned, Jack grabs that bottle again and starts to pound it some more." Maurice pretended again he had the bottle like Jack did.

"She turns around just after Jack sets the bottle down and picks it up to make the second drink. When she's got the two drinks all mixed, she sets them down in front of us. As she turns to put the sugar and honey away you can only imagine what my father-in-law did again," Maurice said proudly.

Before Clair could say a word, Maurice said, "Yup, he grabbed the whisky bottle for the third time and really puts a hurtin' on it this time. There were tears running right down his face he was chugging it so hard," Maurice said, just about yelling at this point.

Clair chuckled at the thought of his old friend. He knew him well and didn't doubt one part of the story.

"So, we finish the second drink," Maurice said, "and Jack yells, 'Harriet! Come fix us another drink!' Harriet comes tearing in from the other room, mad! She yells, 'Just look at you, Jack Farley, you've only had two small drinks and you're falling down drunk! You ain't getting no more!'"

Maurice was just about inconsolable he was laughing so hard. Both Clair and Dana were laughing too. Clair at the antics told of an old friend, and Dana at the antics of a new one.

The storyteller was as funny as the stories he told. Just as the laughter started to subside, Barbara returned to the porch carrying a tray with three bowls.

"You sure I can't get you anything, Maurice?" she asked.

"No, thank you," he replied. "I'm out of beer and it's time to go home. Been gone all week, you know," he said, as if they had forgotten he had mentioned that earlier.

"Well stop in again," Clair said, as both men stood to shake hands.

They watched as Maurice made his way unsteadily down the porch steps.

"I will," Maurice said, as he made his way to his car, calling over his shoulder, "Barbara it was nice to see you again, and a pleasure to meet you, David," apparently forgetting Dana's name.

"Night," they both yelled out in unison.

When the taillights got to the end of the drive Barbara turned to Clair, who still had a smile on his face.

"I'm so glad you don't drink," she said.

Chapter 17

The hay was ready to bale. Dana was surprised how different the twenty-acre meadow looked from when he last saw it just a few hours before. Going from a scattered mess of cut grass strewn throughout the field, drying in the sun, to the neat, orderly windrows now being raked in long snaking rows that followed the contour of the field's boundary, made the meadow look clean.

Clair was busy mowing the next field, so Dana looked for Robert, the eldest of the Rabideau brothers, for direction.

How many brothers are there? he wondered. They seemed to be everywhere, and none were standing still. Some were moving wagons, there was one raking the hay, a couple were poring over the baler, getting it ready. Dana would count them later.

The whole scene reminded Dana of the honey bee colony Clair had showed him in the maple grove. There were thousands and thousands of bees, all doing their own tasks but with one single mission: survival. The colony also had saved the life of the dying maple where the bees had made their home. Dana found that ironic, because normally that would be a tree he and Clair would have cut down, but because of the presence of the hive, the dead tree was saved.

Robert was one of the two men working to ready the baler. Dana walked towards them, stopping before he got in their way.

The baler was hitched to a red tractor that provided the baler's power through the tractor's power take off system, or p.t.o., as it was known for short. It was universal to all tractors and equipment.

Kachunka, Kachunka, Kachunka, the baler seemed to say, every time the p.t.o of the tractor turned the heavy flywheel of the baler, putting all the working parts in motion.

Dana and Robert made eye contact. Robert had both hands buried in the back of the baler but gave a smile and uptick of his chin as to say, 'give me a minute.'

Working with him, holding a big spool of twine, was an older version of Robert. Probably his father or an uncle, Dana thought.

Dana watched what the others were doing, then turned back towards the baler when he heard a cover slam shut. Robert was walking towards him. He was a rugged-looking man, though not practically tall, probably five foot eight, but with broad shoulders and a bulging chest. The hair that showed from the edges of his cap was jet black. His forearms were noticeably large and all his exposed skin was a weathered brown.

"Hi, Dana," he said in a heavy French accent, sticking out a massive paw to shake his hand.

"Hi, Robert," Dana replied, returning the handshake. Dana's hand felt small and weak compared to Roberts's powerful grasp.

"Just checking where you want me," Dana said.

"I tink I will have you in da hay barn as soon as we get a load," Robert directed.

Dana loved the way the French Canadian accent didn't allow the pronunciation of the th's when they spoke.

"My Fatter will do da baling onto da wagon and I will stack da 'ay. You can 'elp my brodders unload and stack in da barn," he continued.

"Day know what to do," Robert said. "Da same as last year."

"Michel," Robert yelled, and waved over an even younger and slightly smaller version of himself, but with blond hair. Dana guessed that the brother's name was Michael, but with the accent sounded like Michel.

Dana shook hands with him as they both said hello.

They both turned to Robert when he spoke.

"Dis is Dana. He owns da farm dat was Joe Lanou's dat we hay. You show him what to do."

"Ok," Michael said with a smile towards Dana, "You come wit me."

Dana turned to thank Robert but he had already left. He was ten feet away, hitching a hay wagon to the back of the baler. Dana turned to follow Michael. He was already ten feet away in the other direction, heading towards the barn.

Man, Dana thought, *these guys don't stay still for a second,* as he jogged a few steps to catch up.

They walked to the front of the hay barn where there were two more guys standing over a long hay elevator with a rusty fifty-five gallon barrel next to it. They were tying a rope to the end of the elevator closest to the barn.

"Bernard, Gaston," Michael said. "Dis here is Dana. He lives here and is going to 'elp." Dana quickly shook hands with both and the pair went right back to work after acknowledging him.

"Dana," Michael said, "what we need to do is set dis elevator up so dat it is in da 'ay barn and da 'ay can drop dare so we can stack it." Michael was pointing to the upper level of the hay barn where months before both Clair and Barbara had shown him the hay piled high.

The little hay left there now had been moved and stacked over the heifer barn.

"We will put dis end on dis barrel after," Michael directed, pointing at the end that would be sticking out of the barn.

That explained what the barrel was for.

The elevator was thirty feet long and looked like a fire truck ladder but with deeper sides. It had a chain with hooks every couple feet that ran the length of the elevator and then circled back underneath it. The hooks would catch the bale when it was placed on the elevator and the bale would ride to the end where it would dump off as the chain circled back underneath.

The end of the elevator that would be propped up on the barrel had an electric motor with a chain and sprocket, not unlike a bicycle set-up.

The hay wagons would be pulled up to the barrel. One person placing bales on the elevator could usually keep the three guys in the hay loft busy, depending on how and where the bales were being stacked.

Now the elevator had to be lifted into place.

Michael asked Dana to grab the corner opposite him. Bernard and Gaston had already positioned themselves on the front corners that would be up in the loft and to where they were tying the rope when Dana was introduced to them.

It was all there as the four of them picked it up on Michael's command and moved towards the barn. They set it down when Barnard hollered, "Good!" Bernard and Gaston raced for the ladder and were in the loft in seconds.

Dana followed Michael to the end where the rope was tied. Michael grabbed the rope and heaved it up to the loft. Gaston grabbed it out of the air and pulled up the slack.

"Here, Dana, grab dat corner and we'll lift as they pull," Michael said.

Dana grabbed his corner and together with the boys up in the loft pulling, that end of the elevator was lifted into place. Michael spoke in French to the boys in the loft as Dana followed Michael out towards the end which had to be set on the barrel.

"Grab that barrel," Michael directed Dana. Dana rolled the barrel towards the elevator.

Bernard and Gaston were sliding down the elevator feet first from the hay barn, careful to keep the rears above the hooks.

"That's quicker than using the ladder," Dana commented to Michael. Michael had seen it a thousand times before and barely looked that way.

"Ok, ready," he said to Dana. "Let's lift dis up and set it on da barrel."

Dana grabbed the corner and both grunted as they lifted it up. Bernard had a board in his hand and was ready to place it across the barrel Gaston was maneuvering.

Gaston must have been taking too long, as Michael barked something to him in French that sped him up. They lowered the elevator onto the board.

Michael plugged the electric motor into an extension cord. The chain sprang to life. They were ready for hay.

They didn't have to wait long.

As soon as the elevator was working, Michael had jumped on a tractor with an empty wagon behind it. He returned just a few minutes later with a load of hay stacked about eight rows high.

He expertly pulled the load up to the elevator.

"Let's go," he ordered.

In seconds Bernard and Gaston were scurrying up the elevator.

"Dana," Michael said in a less threatening tone. "Why don't you work with tose boys for a few loads until you get use to what goes on, den we can switch around a little."

"Ok," Dana replied.

He took a look at the elevator but headed for the ladder in the barn instead.

Just like Michael said, I'll get use to what goes on den I'll try dat elevator, chuckling to himself as he climbed the ladder to the hay loft.

Chapter 18

The bales kept coming.

Michael unloaded the wagons and was able to keep the elevator full, almost bale to bale. Bernard and Gaston positioned Dana at the end of the elevator. Dana would grab the bales as they fell off and toss them to Gaston. Gaston would throw them to Bernard, where he would stack them on their side, cut side down. The cut side was where the baler cut the hay and the bales seemed to stack better and tighter with that edge on the bottom.

It was hot in the hay barn. The sun beat on the tin roof, heating the interior to well over one hundred degrees and there was no breeze. It was like being in an oven. As hot as it was, it seemed good to sweat. It was good, hard work, and with the Rabideau brothers around, fun.

Dana had spent most of his time with Clair and Barbara. It was always good times, he enjoyed their company immensely. It did seem nice for a change to be around a group of younger men more his age, although Bernard and Gaston were twenty-five and twenty-six years old. Age didn't matter much on the farm if you could do the work, and the three became fast friends.

Dana found out that the Rabideaus were sixteen kids strong. That amazed him. *Sixteen brothers and sisters,* he thought. *How the heck do you think up all those names?* There were nine boys and seven girls, with the youngest being sixteen and the oldest, Robert, was forty. A couple of the girls were nuns and one of their older brothers was a priest. The three of them lived in Montreal, and would occasionally come home together for the holidays.

Six of the brothers still lived on the farm, which was one of the largest around with nearly a hundred milk cows. Dana had learned most of that from just one load. When the last bale dropped off the elevator, Michael shut it off from below.

"Come on," Gaston said to Dana as the two brothers jumped on the elevator to slide down.

Dana thought about it for a second, but decided to take the ladder instead.

When he reached the floor, Dana was surprised how cool the breeze felt against his sweat soaked shirt. It felt nice as he held his arms out straight and let the breeze cool him. "Ahhhhhhh," he said out loud to no one but himself, "that feels good."

It was hot out but a lot hotter in the hay barn.

Dana could see the brothers in the milk house and followed them in. They were taking turns drinking from the spring pipe that dumped water into the cement tub that held the full milk cans.

"It is cold," Bernard said, moving over to let Dana drink.

Dana took his hat off and bent over to drink from the pipe. He took several large gulps and then put his head underneath the pipe, letting the chilled water run through his hair and down his back. It seemed days ago that he was swimming in the river instead of this morning.

How good would that be right now? he thought. Dana stepped away to let the brothers drink again.

Gaston stood up with his head cocked. "He's coming," he said, and took one last, quick drink. Bernard did the same and followed his brother out the door. Dana followed suit, taking one last drink from the pipe before following the boys to the hay barn. Michael appeared around the corner of the barn with another full load just as Dana reached the ladder. He was in place when the elevator started again.

It was a load every half hour. One hundred and forty bales per load. It didn't seem at first to add up much, but by six o'clock there was a noticeable pile started.

Barbara had put the cows in and readied the milkers. Dana was going to have to take a break from haying to milk. Clair was still in the other field conditioning what he had mowed. It worked out fine because the younger brother who had been raking the hay into windrows, whom Dana hadn't met yet, had finished and would take Dana's place in the hay barn.

By the time Dana had finished milking it was after eight pm. The boys had to stop baling as the dew had set and was making the bales damp. If the bales were put in the barn too damp it would start a fire by spontaneous combustion, a natural process that heated the bales until they burst into flames.

Clair was done with his field work and was talking with Robert outside their pickup truck door by the main road. Dana walked up to the window to join them.

"My brodders say you did good," Robert said to Dana.

Dana mumbled a "thanks", embarrassed to be singled out from the efforts of the others. Sitting in the passenger seat was Robert's father, Jean-Paul, who had done all the baling.

The patriarch of the family, he didn't speak much English, in fact preferred not to. He let Robert do the business dealings as well, and had passed the reins to him a few years before.

Robert respected him, as all the brothers did, and it was apparent that what he said, went. It was all based on respect, their whole being. That's what Dana had come to realize as he was doing chores. After working with the Rabideaus for only one day he'd come to understand they were like the honey bees in the maple grove, everyone had a job to do. Do it and do it well and everybody would survive. Not doing it wasn't an option.

Chapter 19

Dana and Duke squeezed through the barbed wire fence to gather the cows, scattered throughout the day pasture, for the evening milking. They were met by a few of the older cows making their way towards the barn, more willing to be relieved of the heavy load of milk stored in their bulging udders then some of the younger ones who didn't produce as much and probably were not as uncomfortable. Most of the cows had a sense of what time they would be pushed to the barn, but that still didn't mean they would come on their own. There were always stragglers who were not going to be cheated out of getting herded.

Dana looked towards the end of the pasture where there was a clump of cedar trees. There was a commotion. A group of three or four cows were darting to and fro amongst the trees. *Is it horseflies biting them?* Dana wondered

Dana studied the situation as he made his way up the slight hill along with Duke, who had darted ahead, with his ears pointed forward and his gaze fixed on the group of agitated cows. *Something certainly has them stirred up,* Dana thought.

Duke had now reached the tree line and disappeared into the cover of the cedar branches. A couple barks rang from within as Duke identified the problem. Some more commotion followed and the mystery was solved as the group of cows came charging out of the trees followed by a bull, with Duke triumphantly following behind. Dana watched as the cows ran towards the barn, kicking their heels up in their excitement with their tails held high, with the somewhat smaller, scraggly-looking brown bull chasing from behind.

I wonder where he came from? Dana took a quick look in the trees to make sure he had all the cows before heading towards the barn.

Duke had not waited and was following the unwanted visitor.

Dana could see Clair standing at the gate, ready to open it to let the cows cross the road and then enter the barn through the open door.

By the time he made it to the road Clair was closing the gate. The cows and bull had disappeared inside. Duke was standing in the doorway to keep any from escaping.

"Whose bull do you think?" Dana asked.

"I'd say by looking at him and his condition he belonged to the Browns," Clair replied. "He's awful scrawny. Let's get those cows tied up before they destroy the barn and then we'll herd him into the heifer barn and tie him up."

The Browns owned a small rundown farm a half mile south of the Phillips'. They had a collection of animals and kids; the exact amount of each was probably unknown even to them, as it was hard to tell where the barn and house were divided.

Dana had seen some of the kids walking by on their way to town, but they were shy and mainly kept to themselves. They still milked by hand, and even though the electric lines ran by their property, had only a few light bulbs scattered throughout the house and barn. The family didn't own a vehicle, but had a tractor. It wasn't uncommon to see all of them gathered in the back of a trailer being pulled by the tractor when the family wanted to go somewhere together. They were subsistent farmers. Long before any government assistance, what they had was what they earned or raised. Other than a little flour and sugar, not much was bought from a store. The same, though, could be said of a lot of the country folk. Just most had more than the Browns.

With the cows tied, Dana and Clair, with the help of Duke, pushed the bull into the heifer barn as planned. Dana was able to get a halter on him.

"Why don't you start milking and I'll run up to the Browns and ask them if they're missing their bull," Clair said. Dana agreed and turned to towards the cow barn, but not before witnessing Clair kicking some hay towards the stunted bull. Dana smiled as he walked away. *The old man can't stand to see a neglected animal,* he thought.

Dana was half done milking when Clair returned. "It's theirs," he announced, before disappearing in front of the cows to grain them. A few minutes later, when Dana was lugging two pails of milk to the milk house, Clair and he met again. "They'll be over after chores to get him," he said.

The two finished chores and were letting the cows out to the night pasture, which was on the barn side of the road so when morning milking came, they didn't have to worry about trying to cross the cows across a dark road in the early morning hour, when they heard a tractor coming from the Brown's way.

Dana looked over his shoulder as the last of the cows made their way through the gate.

The small red tractor with well worn tires appeared to have grown appendices, as everywhere he looked seemed to have a body hanging off from it. Dana counted five people including the driver, as the loud tractor that was missing its exhaust stack rolled to a stop.

All the bodies, dressed alike in worn, ill-fitting, faded denim and flannel, piled off the tired tractor and stood in line. Their dirty faces showed no expressions, and except for the father, avoided any eye contact, the bills of their soiled caps pulled down low on their foreheads.

Dana guessed the youngest to be about five years old and the oldest was probably a few years younger than he, at fourteen.

"Where is that wandering son-of-a gun?" the father asked, looking towards the barn and then back towards Clair and Dana.

"Got the horny little fella captured in the heifer barn," Clair answered, pointing towards the wide open double doors of the hay barn which led to the heifer barn. Dana led the way, with the tribe of the Browns following.

"You know," said the father, "I bought that bull from Booze about three months ago and he was the most worthless bull I'd ever seen."

"How so?" asked Clair.

"Well," he answered, "he wouldn't breed my cows. More afraid of them than anything. He'd run right away from them if they were in standing heat," the father declared.

"Really," Clair said in disbelief. "He was sure trying to mount anything that moved when we saw him."

"That's the way he's been since Doc Stevens gave him that stuff. Can't keep him home! This is the third time this week I've had to haul him home. Been trying to breed everything in the county," the father exclaimed.

"What stuff did the Doc give him?" Clair asked.

"Well," the father answered, "It's a powder that comes in a five gallon pail and comes with a little scoop. Doc said to give it to him mixed in his drinking water once a day. Just a scoop. I give him two. Probably I'm going to have to cut him back."

"Probably you should," Clair agreed, "if he's going to act like that. What the hell is it, anyways?

"Don't have any idea," answered father Brown, "but it tastes a lot like peppermint!"

CHAPTER 20

Haying took fifteen days and Clair was pleased. 8,889 bales were now in the barn, according to the counter on the baler. There didn't seem to be an empty spot anywhere in the hay barn.

"Now if the world goes to hell we'll still be okay," Clair said to Dana. "We would at least be able to last another year."

Dana had thought the comment funny, but it made sense. Short of the barn burning down, there wasn't much that would keep them from surviving. The water flowed off the mountain to the house and barn, they could milk cows by hand if need be and the cellar would be full of wood. It was a good feeling.

The wood business was also going well. Dana had nearly eighty cords piled behind the workshop and planned to have a total of a hundred by the end of August, before school started again. That gave him better than four weeks to get it done.

At $30 per cord that was enough to take care of this year's taxes and pay some back to Barbara and Clair for what they had lent him.

There was one thing, however, that confused Dana. He knew what he was able to draw for wood when Clair wasn't able. But on the days Clair did draw while Dana did chores, Clair would have almost twice the amount of wood pulled to the splitter. It didn't make sense.

Yes, Dana was new to the tractor and chain saw. And yes, maybe he was too careful, but it didn't add up. There was no way the old man could get that much more done by himself. There had to be someone helping him, but who?

Dana thought he had seen different boot prints in some mud along one of the wood roads but he didn't think much about it. He had also noticed things out of place when he knew he had been the last one there; the wood peaveys not where he left them, and fuel cans moved. *I'll have to pay more attention,* he told himself. *It probably was the stranger again.* Dana had let the opportunity pass last time without saying anything. He wouldn't pass on the next chance. But the opportunity had to present itself.

As Dana stood at the splitter, he was marveling at how well it worked. He watched as another log was pushed down the rail towards him. He pulled down on the handle of the circular saw blade when the log reached its mark, and watched as the blade easily cut the wood to length. He then watched as the pieces cut a few cycles before made their way to the wedge splitter, where they were split into quarters and fell into the trailer below. The hardest part was to roll the logs to the splitter, but even that was an easy process now.

Dana's mind kept drifting away from the task at hand. He had to find a way, without being discovered, of finding out who was helping Clair, if in fact there was anybody at all. He had thought about just coming out and asking, but had lost his nerve more than once. Besides, what if nobody was helping? Clair would be insulted.

Dana worked the next log into place with the peavey. He pushed the button and watched as the forks lifted the log off the ground then deposited it, with a *Ka-thunk!* onto the splitter. His stomach gave a growl as he snuck a look at his watch; almost noon. He would finish this one and break for lunch.

He felt a smile come over his face as he thought about what he planned to do during lunch. He had brought his fish pole. That big lunker of a fish he saw when he last went swimming didn't stand a chance.

Clair had helped him set up his pole and even gave him his own wicker fish basket to use, complete with a compartment for his hooks and sinkers, to keep any fish in, should he catch any.

The two of them dug for worms below the barn where the manure had seeped from the cellar. "Worms like shit," Clair told Dana.

Clair instructed him to use the dung fork, a fork farmers had used to load the manure spreaders before tractors had buckets on them. "The dung fork won't cut your worms in half," he explained. "The bigger the worm, the bigger the fish." They had gotten some big worms. Dana stored them in a coffee can.

Dana chuckled out loud thinking about his boasting to Barbara this morning. "You had better plan on trout for supper," he warned her.

"I'll take some chicken out, just in case," she chided him back.

Dana pulled the handle for the circular saw one last time as the piston reached its end. He hit the button to shut the spinning blade off and then walked over to shut the machine down. Jumping off the platform, he walked the few steps to where his lunch basket lay in the shade along with his worms in the can. Dana shook the dirt to expose the slimy looking worms all bunched in a ball. *Yuk*, he thought, *I'm sure glad I'm not a fish!*

He made his way towards the lunch rock, grabbing his pole leaned up against the splitter as he passed. Dana set the basket on the rock and his worms next to it.

He shook the dirt again in the can and reached for one of the plump worms. He grabbed one and tugged it slightly, pulling it away from the entangled pile. The worm slithered in his hand as he held onto it with his forefinger and thumb close to one of its ends, readying the hook with his other. He slid the hook into the worm, making it squirm more. Hooking it three times, the worm was securely fastened.

The worm dangled at the end of the line as Dana flipped open the bale of the reel.

Picking a spot in the pool where the water tumbled from above, he cast the worm and admired his work as the line whirled from the reel and the worm landed where he had intended it to. He waited a second after the worm splashed into the turbulent water and sunk towards the bottom. The strong current pushed the line downstream, towards the deep pool. Dana turned the handle on the reel, setting the line.

He no more than set the pole against the rock with its tip hanging over the edge, when the tip dove towards the water as a fish struck the worm. Dana reached quickly for the pole, surprised, and cranked on the handle, taking up the slack line. He felt nothing.

Boy that was fast, he thought, as he reeled in the line to check his worm. The hook was bare.

Dana baited the hook again. Picking out the same spot, he repeated his first cast. It landed as it had before. *Be ready, be ready,* he thought as he reeled the excess line, excited, waiting for the bump that he hoped would come.

Wham! The trout hit and Dana flicked up his rod tip. He had one!

Dana could feel the fish pulling and could see his pole bending in an arc as the fish raced first towards the falls, and then back downstream. It didn't feel particularly big. Dana kept the line tight and slowly reeled, straining to glimpse the fish in the clear stream, to see just how big it was.

The fish fought harder as it neared the edge. There! Dana could now see it. He hoisted his prize onto the gravel shore. It was about 8 inches, he guessed. Not the monster he was looking for, but it would be good eating.

The fish jiggled and shook as Dana guided his hand down the line towards it. He wrapped his hand around the small trout, holding it firmly enough to take the hook out of its lower lip but not wanting to squish it. It was a brook trout. Dana could tell by the speckled orange and red spots on its side. Its belly had traces of pink that blended into its lower fins. It was beautifully marked.

Dana dropped the fish through the square hole in the top of the wicker basket. He thought about how excited he was as he quickly baited his hook. He was actually shaking a little as he was readying to cast again. *This is fun,* he thought as his worm splashed at the base of the falls and disappeared below the surface. It would be even more fun to catch that big one. But it wasn't to happen.

Dana caught his limit of twelve fish, losing very few worms. All the fish were between eight and ten inches. It would be plenty for their supper.

Dana took out his jack knife from his front pocket and cleaned the fish. When he was done he put them back in the wicker basket and set the basket in the shallow edge of the stream, keeping the fish cool. Barbara's chicken would have to wait another day.

It was time to go back to work.

You know what you should do first? Dana thought. *You should probably eat your lunch!* He had forgotten to in all his excitement.

Chapter 21

It was at breakfast, near the end of July, when Clair suggested that maybe they could start chores a little earlier that night. An all-star baseball team from Sherbrooke, Canada had challenged Ethenburg's undefeated men's town team to a game to be held on the common. First pitch was to be at 6:30. They would play until dark or seven innings, whichever came first.

Barbara and Dana readily agreed. Clair must have really wanted to go. He usually wasn't up for much after chores except for sitting on the porch, reading the paper or maybe working in the garden some.

"I'll have a light supper ready before you two start chores," Barbara offered. "And maybe I'll make some ice cream today that we can have after the game. Dana, maybe you could ask Polly and David down after to enjoy it with us."

"Yup, I will," Dana responded. He hadn't seen his aunt and uncle for a while and it would be great to spend some time with them. He doubted whether David would come, but he was sure Polly would.

Of all the years that Dana had lived in Mill village, he had only seen a couple games played. Not many of the mill crowd would venture up the hill. A few times Polly had, but they had watched from afar, not sitting on the bleachers as they were usually full and Polly was uncomfortable.

Dana could remember the festive atmosphere. People would applaud or cheer loudly a good play or a timely hit or maybe even a home run. The CRACK! of the wooden bats seemed to echo off the houses and businesses surrounding the common.

The vehicles would also park around the village green, surrounding the common with colorful iron. No fences needed. Hit it over the vehicles and it was out of play, be it a home run or a foul ball, depending on the direction.

Every game it was sure to happen, a foul ball would fall from the sky amongst the vehicles and everybody would await the Bang! or the Crash! of someone's fender or windshield. The crowd would hold their breath, then ohhh! and ahhhh! and a curious few would venture over to see if it was their vehicle or not. Not to worry, the kids who ran and chased one another and the foul balls would report back in short order who the unlucky one was.

Sometimes the game would be delayed as the baseballs were in short supply and too many foul balls in a row would slow the game, until the balls were chased down and returned.

The players of both teams were smartly dressed in colorful uniforms of whites or yellows or tans, with black or red numbers on the backs of their jerseys and the name of their team emblazoned on their fronts with matching ball caps. Some of the more affluent teams would even have their last names sewn on the back above their numbers. Their socks were pulled up high almost to their knees, into which their baggy uniform pant bottoms were stylishly tucked.

The umpires, usually two, were dressed in blue, and most were older, retired players. Each team would usually supply one umpire, with the home team calling the balls and strikes.

After the game was over the home team would "pass the hat" and the few dollars collected would pay the umpires, buy a few baseballs and sometimes, if it was an especially generous crowd, buy a little beer for the players who stayed around after the game.

The crowds were people of the home team mostly, but it wasn't uncommon for the good teams to have a large following of their own. Behind each team bench sat the wooden bleachers packed with people supporting their team. Just as many people sat on the hoods of their cars or in the backs of their trucks surrounding the playing field and would honk their horns if they liked what they saw.

It would be fun, and maybe Dana would even get to see some of his classmates he hadn't seen since school let out. He only worked until noon on his wood. He wanted to be home in plenty of time to start chores early.

After lunch he helped Clair fix some of the barbed wire fences around the hay fields. The fields had started to grow back and Clair was thinking about putting the cows in the first field they had hayed.

"I'd like it if we could wait another week to let them grow," Clair said, "but their pastures are getting thin." They were still working on the fences at three o'clock, when Barbara called to them for supper.

She had the picnic table on the front lawn, under the big maple, set up for their light supper. She was busy shooing away flies when they pulled up with the tractor and small trailer that Clair used for fencing.

"What's for supper?" Clair asked as he climbed off the tractor.

"Oh, I had to use up the rest of that turkey we had the other night so I made some biscuits and gravy," Barbara answered.

Clair looked at the table full of food and shook his head. "I thought you said we were going to have a light supper." He grabbed the wet towel Barbara had brought with her for the men to wipe their hands with.

"Well, you might be hungry after the game and this will be easy to heat up," Barbara answered, undeterred in her fly-clearing task.

"What, and miss out on the ice cream?" Clair bantered, fully understanding that Barbara had never known the meaning of "light" for any meal.

Clair tossed the wet towel to Dana and took his seat at the table.

Barbara took the cover off the biscuits and passed them to Clair, who took a couple and broke them open, spreading them out on his plate. She passed the biscuits to Dana, who did the same as Clair. Barbara covered them up, shooing the flies away again. "I'll tell you what, these flies seem to know...." Her voice tailed off, not talking to anyone in particular.

Clair held out his plate to Barbara after smearing butter on his biscuits. Barbara lifted the cover off the black cast iron kettle as the steam shot up, and ladled a generous portion of turkey gravy with chunks of carrots, onion and peas and a few baby red potatoes mixed in.

"Looks good," Clair praised as he mixed the gravy, biscuits and butter together.

Barbara fixed Dana's plate and then her own.

Duke appeared from down where they had fixed the fence and waited patiently off to Barbara's side. She lifted the cover to the biscuits and tossed him one. Duke caught it mid air and gulped it down it one motion.

"I think if he could talk he wouldn't have any idea what you just fed him, he ate it so fast," Clair said, adding, "I don't think it touched his taste buds."

Barbara agreed, with Dana quipping, "I know how he feels! This is good."

The three laughed as Barbara responded, "I'm glad you like it. It's just heated up leftovers."

They made some small talk until Barbara asked Clair, "Why don't you take me to town first and then we could ride down and pick up Polly and David, if he'll come, and I'll set with them on the bleachers so they will feel comfortable until you guys get there."

"Sounds okay to me," Clair said. "Why don't you plan for ten of six. Dana will be finished by 6:15 and I'll just swing right back and pick him up."

"That okay with you Dana?" Clair asked, as Barbara looked on.

"Sounds like a plan, but again, I wouldn't plan on David going," Dana said.

"I didn't figure so but he's more than welcome if he wants to," Barbara said as she started to pick up dinner. Dana stood to help. Barbara shooed him away like she had done with the flies.

"You've got plenty to do in the barn. I can take care of this."

Dana left to get the cows with Duke following. They were scattered throughout the pasture and seemed confused at the earlier than normal time. Dana herded them towards the barn with Duke's help. Clair was standing at the gate and opened it when the last cow straggled up. Both started chores, with Dana doing the milking and Clair feeding the cows their grain.

On cue, Clair left to take Barbara to town and was back to pick up Dana as they has discussed earlier.

"Did David come?" Dana asked as he got in the truck.

"Nope," Clair answered, "but Polly was happy."

The truck lumbered towards town. When they reached the lane that divided the two farms Dana realized Duke wasn't following.

"Where's the dog?" he quizzed Clair.

"I told him to stay when I brought up Barbara and he went sulking off, mad," Clair answered.

That was one smart, independent dog, Dana thought. He still had never followed him or even seen where he snuck off to at night. *Someday, maybe when there's snow on the ground, I'll follow him.*

He certainly liked to lay in the ledges where it was cool while Dana split wood. He guessed that the loud processor and chainsaw probably hurt his ears because he never stayed around when either were running.

The truck drew nearer the common. It was wall to wall vehicles. Not since the Church Fair had Dana seen so many. Clair turned right and circled the common, looking for a place to park.

"A lot of people," he said, as he drove by Rob's market and then back towards Johnson's store, finally finding a parking place to the right of the store, below the big painting.

"Not so bad of a spot," Clair said, seemingly happy that they only had a hundred yard walk to the bleachers.

Dana could hear the POP!, Pop!, Pop! of the baseballs as they struck the leather gloves of the men in uniforms warming up, playing catch. There was a buzz in the air, like electricity. The voices of people grew louder as they approached the field. The two walked towards the bleachers. Dana scanned the crowd, looking for familiar faces.

He did see a couple of his classmates further over behind the back stop and gave them a short wave to acknowledge them. He would walk around a little later after spending some time with Aunt Polly.

Dana rounded the front of the home crowd bleachers, behind the team bench, and located Polly and Barbara. They had seen him first and were smiling and waving to him.

He turned to look for Clair but saw he had gotten held up, talking to somebody Dana didn't recognize.

Dana excused himself to the people who were seated as he stepped up onto the first row of bleachers and made his way to the two women. He bent down and kissed his aunt on the cheek, as she hugged him with one arm, remaining seated. Dana sat beside her.

"Long time, no see," he said to her as they both grinned broadly at one another.

"I know," Polly responded, "too long, I've missed you."

"I've missed you guys too," Dana said, wanting to include David.

"David said to say hi," Polly said, picking up on Dana's response. "You know this isn't his thing." She gestured at the crowd.

"I know," Dana answered. "I probably would have dropped over dead had I seen him here."

"So what have you been up to?" his aunt asked him.

Dana told her about the wood processor, driving the tractor, milking cows, haying and the Rabideau brothers and everything else that came to mind as he spoke excitedly, almost forgetting to take breaths, oblivious to the crowd and goings on around him. He told Polly of the money that he had earned to pay this year's taxes on his land and of the extra that he was planning to give to Clair and Barbara to pay back what they had lent him. It was as though he and Polly were the only ones there.

Polly listened intently, the broad smile never leaving her face, asking question as Dana filled her in about life with the Phillips' and the farm. It was only when the umpire hollered loudly, "Play Ball" that they remembered where they were. Dana turned his attention to the field as Ethenburg's pitcher was in his windup.

"STRIKE!" yelled the umpire, Fats Royea, as the ball smacked the catcher's mitt, sparking approval from everybody on the home team side.

Dana looked for Clair. He finally saw him on his right, sitting on the far side of Barbara.

He and Polly had been so caught up in catching up that he hadn't seen him make his way up the bleachers.

Dana thought how good it was to see his aunt. As much as Clair and Barbara had done in a short amount of time, Polly and David had been there for the long haul.

Polly sat next to her nephew, surprised by the changes of his appearance. He had, in a few short months, matured. He was a very handsome boy, she admired, as she stole glances at him. The deep bronze skin of his arms accentuated his long forearms, leading up to his developed biceps showing from beneath the cuffs of his tee shirt.

His broadening shoulders that she lay her cheek against leading up to the smooth lines of his face with his bright white teeth and tufts of longer blond hair curling out below his cap would surely soon catch the attention of some young girl's eyes. In fact, he had, as Polly noticed a couple giggling girls about his age, sneaking peeks and trying hard not to be noticed or maybe just trying hard to be, standing off to their left.

The poor boy, she thought, smiling from within, *He doesn't have a clue.*

Polly sat a little straighter. She could be proud of what she had accomplished.

Polly had worked hard to keep Dana above the ruckuses that could happen in Mill village. Not that she could ever be ashamed of the task she and David undertook, raising her brother's son, knowing they had tried their best. The shame could have come from what they might not have accomplished had they not tried so hard. David was a part as well. He never second-guessed her and when it came to Dana, always did as she had asked of him.

Dana was a special child, Polly thought. Not that most people in parenting positions wouldn't think that of their own. But he had tried hard too. Almost as if he understood from that first night when the Trooper brought the three of them home from the Town Hall, that he and the McCays would be judged by the "others."

Polly still vividly remembered the gasps from the town folk when Mr. Williams, the moderator, instructed the Trooper to take them home. *Let them gasp now,* she thought triumphantly.

The first strike was about the only good thing that happened for the home team. Sherbrooke scored three runs in the first, a couple more in the second and by the third inning, had put the game out of reach, scoring five more.

Sherbrooke's pitcher was too much for the Ethenburg men as he mowed them down with strikeouts, groundouts and pop flies, never letting a runner past second base. The team conceded early, not on the field as they valiantly fought on, but in the passing of the hat, not wanting to let the good opportunity they had with the large crowd pass. There would be extra beer tonight.

Dana excused himself about the fifth inning, telling his aunt and the Phillips' he was going to say hi to a couple friends.

He made his way towards the back stop, careful to slow down before he got there to let a couple girls he had seen watching him catch up.

"Hi, Dana," they said in unison, giggling and hanging on one another.

Dana turned to face them, acting surprised. "Hello, ladies," he responded, which got the girls giggling even more, as he gave them a big smile. Their names were Kathy and Wanda, and they were from his class.

"What are you girls up to?" he asked, disappointed that he had asked such a stupid question.

"Oh, just watching the game," Kathy, the braver one answered, causing still more giggling from the two.

"Wanda! Wanda!" Dana heard someone calling from the stands. Both the girls turned to look at the lady calling out the name.

"Who's that?" Dana asked.

"Oh that's just my stupid mother," Wanda responded, rolling her eyes in disgust. "She hates when I talk to any boys."

The irate mother called out again, "Wanda Jean!" a little sterner this time.

"We have to go," Wanda said.

"We'll see you in school in a couple weeks," Kathy said, as Wanda yelled "Yes, mother," over her shoulder.

"I guess you will," Dana responded, doing the calculation in his head. He didn't correct her that school was still a month away, as he hadn't given school much thought. The girls whirled around, giggling as they left, looking over their shoulders one last time.

Dana watched them leave. *Cute,* he said to himself, *both of them.*

Clair watched Dana from the stands, a little grin on his face.

"And just what are you smirking about?" Barbara said, poking him in the ribs, observing the scene too.

"Nothing," Clair said. "Nothing at all," but his proud smile gave him away.

Chapter 22

Dana now had his driver's license. The State of Vermont allowed anybody who was fourteen years old to drive under someone else's license, provided the license holder was eighteen and accompanied them. At sixteen, which Dana had turned, the State allowed its citizens to get their driver's license.

Clair let Dana to use the Ford truck. *It's a lot easier to drive than any of the two tractors,* Dana thought. He didn't go too far, but since he and Polly had talked at the ball game they both promised to stay in touch more.

Some nights after chores Dana would drive to Mill village to visit her and David. He had brought some brook trout for supper once but usually didn't plan to eat there. Polly and David ate normally around five and to ask them to eat at eight took David out of his routine. David was usually napping in his chair by then.

Dana and Polly would talk softly so as not to disturb him, or quietly play cards or checkers at the kitchen table.

Sometimes when it wasn't too cool and they felt like being louder, they would sit on the front porch after dark, listening to the radio if there was a good signal and just talking and joking with one another, trying to make each other laugh.

Dana would tell about what was happening at the farm, who might have stopped by or what was going on around through the words of the visitors. Polly would do the same, although not much seemed to change in her life.

One night, as the two sat on the porch and it was quiet, Dana asked Polly, "Do you remember the night that I saw a stranger on the neighbor's porch?"

"Yes I do," Polly replied. "He had left some food on their porch as well as ours."

"You said that night that that wasn't the first time you had found food at the front door," Dana reminded Polly.

"Nope," Polly whispered, "it wasn't. There used to be food left there a couple times a month," she said softly.

"Really!" Dana said, surprised. "What would he leave?" he asked curiously.

"Oh, it was different things, most times depending on the seasons," Polly said, thinking back. "Sometimes it was fresh vegetables, or stuff like eggs and bread and butter. Other times when it was cooler he would leave, once in a while, some meat like deer or beef, usually heart or liver," she remembered.

"Does he still?" Dana asked.

"No, he hasn't in a while, not here anyways," Polly said, and then added, "Come to think of it, I don't think he has since you left. I don't know if he has left anything at the other houses since, either. Nobody talks about it. It was only when I went to the neighbors to ask if they were the ones who had left the food on our porch, when I found it the first time years ago, did I realize that he was leaving food on their porch as well. And then you saw him that night on their porch, so I figured that he was still leaving food with them too," Polly explained.

"Has anyone ever seen him?" Dana pressed.

"Nobody has ever said anything, but like I said before, nobody talks about that stuff around here. Nobody likes handouts," Polly said, protecting her pride.

"As far as I know, only you have seen him" she added. "Why do you ask? Have you seen him again?"

"No," Dana replied, "no, I was just curious and wanted to know what you knew," he answered. "Stuff like that interests me, and I guess someday I would love to meet someone like that. Somebody who doesn't care to be famous but just wants to help where he can without trying to embarrass anyone," Dana said stoically.

"Well, he must be a very nice person, or he has problems sleeping," Polly joked, causing them both to burst out laughing, ending the seriousness of their discussion. "Yeah I guess," Dana said, trying to hold it in, which made him laugh harder. Dana had been prepared to tell his aunt more, but thought better of it. He was sure she had told him all she knew.

It was his mystery to figure out. To tell anyone what he had seen through the register might create too much attention, and might expose someone who only chose to be a good person and wanted nothing else because of it. It would also raise questions about Barbara and Clair's involvement, and Dana wasn't willing to do that.

Dana looked at his watch. It was almost ten o'clock and he should be getting home. They both hugged, and Dana kissed her on her cheek.

"Tell David I said goodnight," Dana said, as he turned to walk to the truck.

"I will, and you drive home safe," Polly cautioned.

"Sure thing," Dana said as he climbed in the driver's door and started the truck. Dana put the truck in gear, giving Polly a wave, and drove slowly down the street of Mill village. Most of the houses were dark except for a few scattered lights here and there. The houses were familiar to him and he felt comfortable being there. It was where he was raised.

The houses gave way to piles of lumber stacked on both sides of the road. He remembered not too long ago when he and his friends use to play among the stacks, hide and seek or other games they would invent. It didn't take long for one of the watchmen to scare them off and they would go find somewhere else to play until the next day, when it would happen all over again.

As Dana got closer to the mill the stacks grew deeper and taller, making the road narrower. The piles never seemed to get smaller no matter how much lumber was trucked away. It was a busy place.

Dana could see the mill silhouetted against the full moon sky. He stopped the truck for a moment. It looked scary and dark. A slight breeze moved the branches of the few trees that had survived standing on the corners closest to him. The branches created an illusion in the dark. It looked as though the mill was pulsing, almost like it was breathing. A chill shot up Dana's back as he put the truck in gear and continued on.

I'm lucky, he thought. *Had it not been for my grandfather and Barbara and Clair, in a few more years that's probably where I'd be.*

I wonder if I would ever have known the difference?

Chapter 23

Dana reached his goal of a hundred cords of wood a week before school started. *A hundred cords,* he thought. *That is awesome!* It certainly didn't seem possible that he would ever reach it when he had first started. He thought back to when months ago he had stacked the first cord. Being the driest it was the first to go, but the posts that marked where it had sat were still there. How long ago it seemed.

He had learned a lot in a short time. He now was sure he understood the commitment one made when one wanted to live off the land; it was seven days a week, three hundred sixty-five days a year.

It seemed odd, though. As tough as farming was it didn't seem like work. Maybe just the surroundings Dana was in made that difference, or maybe one summer just wasn't enough for the negatives to show.

Certainly Clair and Barbara helped make it different. They made farming look easy. Even at their age, they seemed to be having fun.

The love and respect they showed for one another and those around them was obvious. They had pride in what they accomplished and were proud of the way they raised their livestock and cared for their land and kept their buildings up.

Both had their roles to perform to make the farm work and they did them well. Their support for one another was unwavering. Dana knew they were super people. Whatever it was, Dana had certainly learned a lot about himself.

A year before, if someone had asked him what he wanted to do with his life, Dana would not have been able to answer. He wouldn't have understood he had a choice. He certainly had matured through the summer, but he had always been mature beyond his years.

Now he was sure what his future would be, but he also understood it could be whatever he wanted it to be. It was his decision to make.

A few days before school, Clair, Barbara and he had gone to Oldport, a city thirteen miles north of them that bordered the lake, to buy him some new clothes. In all his years he had never had new clothes of his own. Polly had always made sure he was well dressed, certainly as well as anybody else, but they were hand-me-downs.

Dana wasn't sure he knew what he was most proud of when they were on their way home, his new wardrobe or the fact when it came time to pay he was able to pull out his wallet and pay for everything himself. He had even waved off Clair when he insisted on paying.

Only after, when he was home laying his new clothes out on his bed, did it dawn on him that he had to work better than a day to pay for all of what he had purchased, not to mention the wear and tear on the equipment and the wood that was already his.

Thinking about how big a cord of wood was compared to the small pile of what lay before him made Dana chuckle. *I think I'm in the wrong business.*

Dana turned to climb on the tractor. Enough day dreaming. He had a few logs to clean up before he started school.

Thinking about school reminded him that he wasn't sure how he felt about that. He really hadn't devoted any time to considering what high school would be like. A lot of people around him never went to high school. They finished the eighth grade and they were done. That really wasn't an option for him. He would finish high school, he had decided, and then he would think about college. He had made no decisions about that yet, but if he was to wager a bet, he had better get all his learning done before he graduated high school. There certainly was enough to do here to keep him busy. Not to mention that Clair and Barbara would be four years older by the time he finished.

Dana stopped the tractor at the first gate on his and Clair's property line. He must have been deep in thought. He didn't even remember leaving the yard. He jumped down to undo the gate as Duke shot by, taking the lead as he usually did at this point.

Dana pulled the tractor and trailer through. *The heck with it,* he thought. *Today for no reason other than I'm only going to be there a couple hours, I'm going to leave the gates open. Clair will understand.*

Clair had a couple appointments at the farm today. One with the grain salesman to discuss what they would feed for grain this winter, and the other with the veterinarian. They had a sick cow that needed some attention. Otherwise, Dana knew, he'd be here.

It certainly didn't hurt Clair to have an easy day, but he wouldn't allow himself to understand that. It only hurt Barbara, as she was the one who had to put up with him while he waited for the people to show. Clair would pace and complain they were always late even when they showed early. Clair had worked hard this summer. Without his help and guidance Dana would not have been able to process a hundred cords of wood alone.

Dana had tried his best to limit Clair's work. He picked up the slack where Clair allowed. Clair had only milked a couple times after he taught Dana. That alone took a lot of pressure off Clair's knee, not to mention what it did for his shortness of breath. Dana did his best to give him no reason to climb to the hay barn or do anything else that would let him work harder than what he should. The tough part was getting in front of Clair.

Clair was going to do what he wanted to do, when he wanted to do it and nobody was going to tell him different. He had worked all summer in the woods ahead of Dana, dragging logs to the processor. It was a feat that still amazed Dana. He was convinced that he had help but he was unable to confirm it.

The only time that Dana had heard Barbara and Clair argue for real was when she pleaded with him to let the doctor have a look at him. Clair would have none of it, to which Barbara would call him a stubborn old fool.

Dana drove towards the clearing. The leaves of his maples had started to turn their brilliant fall colors in a couple of places, and the canopy he was driving under did seem less full. Summer was coming to an end.

Dana turned an objective eye towards the woods. After scanning the forest he agreed with what his grandfather had told Clair years before. There was enough wood that needed to be cut in his sugar bush so that a healthy maple tree would never have to be cut.

A hundred cord had been harvested and Dana could not see any visible sign that the woods were diminished. He slowed the tractor as he entered the clearing. The panoramic picture in front of him never got old.

He shut the tractor off. He stepped down and walked towards the top of the falls. The water was slightly higher than usual as it had rained the day before. He watched for a moment as the swift moving water dove off the edge of the falls, pounding into the pool below.

He surveyed the flat rocks just inches below the surface that the smugglers had built many years before, making their secret walkway across the top of the falls. *If you didn't know they were there, you'd never know,* Dana thought as he looked to gauge the depth.

He had brought his fish pole today. Today was the day the big trout would not be able to avoid. All summer Dana had tried to catch him. He could catch all the smaller ones he wanted, and did. Every time Dana cast his line towards the falls, the current would push it downstream too fast before his worm had time sink to where the big fish was. The smaller ones would gobble up his worm immediately when it got too far past the deep hole.

Dana had given this a lot of thought. He would stand on the top of the falls and drop his line down into the deep pool. The current would not be able to take his line downstream because he would hold it in place from his strategically placed fishing spot.

Dana took one last look. It was a good plan but first he had to get his work done.

He walked back to the tractor, hopped on and started it. He pulled down the slight hill that led to the wood processor. As he drove by the covered machine sitting on his left, he thought of the good summer they had together. Other than one hydraulic hose that split and had to be replaced, it had operated flawlessly.

He drove past it, further down the hill and then backed the trailer underneath the splitter where he had so many times before. He didn't unhitch it because he only had the few logs to process and none to skid.

He grabbed his fish pole and coffee can of worms from the trailer and walked up the path to the generator. Setting them both down for a moment he peeled the canvas away, exposing the processor. He placed the worms underneath the platform and leaned his pole up against the machine. *Soon that fish will be mine,* he thought, as he adjusted the choke and started the processor.

An hour and a half later Dana was finished sawing and the machine was covered again. He grabbed his poles and worms and walked down to the tractor. *I might as well park this at the top of the falls.*

As he set his worms and pole in the back of the trailer and saw the small pile of wood in the back, he thought about the first load he and Clair had brought home. It was so small they hadn't even bothered to unload it. This one compared to it. *How ironic.*

At the top of the falls Dana stopped. He was excited. He had tried all summer to catch the big fish and now was the time. Dana reached for the biggest worm he could see and pulled it from the slimy ball it was part of. He pierced it with the sharp hook three times, leaving a half inch tail dangling. *That will get his attention.*

Dana looked at the rock platform through the rushing water. He stepped out with one foot cautiously, putting his weight on it, judging if it was safe or not. With one foot on shore and one on the platform, it felt good. Now that his foot broke the mirroring effect of the water, Dana could see that the platform walkway was nearly two feet wide. *Just amazing,* he marveled.

He stepped on with his dry foot. Looking down, he could see the water rushing around his rubber boots. It was only about two inches deep but he could feel the force of the river still. Dana looked across the top of the falls to the other side of the river. It was probably eight paces across. Feeling more comfortable, he took another step. Looking around at the trees and rocks helped as he gained more confidence. *It is better if you don't look down... Two more steps,* he coached himself. They were hard ones, but Dana took them. Now standing in the middle of the river, he turned and faced downstream.

"Who would ever have believed this?" Dana said aloud, as he looked at the crashing water below and followed its path downstream.

Dana readied his pole. He flipped the bale and let his worm drop into the furious white water below him. He waited and watched his line and reeled when he thought his worm was in perfect position. He felt a nudge. His pole bent quickly down. He had one!

Dana could now see he had let his line drift too far downstream. He reeled in his prize, lifting it up over the falls. It was a nice brookie, about nine inches long, but it wasn't what he had come for today. Dana carefully worked the hook out of the colorful little fish and tossed it back in the river behind him. *Go find some new friends,* Dana offered. He walked to the side of the river to bait his hook again. He turned and walked carefully back out with his new fish meal.

This time you need to be about three feet closer to the falls.

Dana got himself comfortable and dropped his line again. When the worm reached the water he counted. *One thousand one, one thousand two,* and then quickly turned his reel, locking the bale. *There, it's right where I wanted.*

Dana waited; nothing, not a bite. He knew the fish was there.

He was gripping the pole tightly in his right hand. He went to switch the pole to his left hand.

As he was transferring the grip the fish hit. *Wham!*

The force surprised Dana and jerked the pole from his hand. Dana, startled, lunged for the pole, losing his footing. His feet shot out from under him as he began to fall backwards.

"Aw, shit!" he yelled, as he put his hands down to try to keep himself from going over the edge.

He fell with a *Bang!* And then it was dark.

Dana could feel somewhere in his mind intense cold as he felt his body being carried away. He was drifting, free, just floating on air. Through a haze he could hear a familiar voice yelling his name, but he couldn't place it.

Now he could see the hat, the odd shape of the stranger's hat outlined in a blurry vision. He still couldn't see his face. It was like the dreams he had of him. He must be dreaming, just go back to sleep. The stranger was now hysterically yelling his name, "No Dana! No Dana! You need to wake up!"

Dana fought the urge but it was just too powerful. He felt his body being tugged and pulled and carried as he drifted into that comfortable place that was calling for him.

Chapter 24

Dana could here soft voices. He recognized Barbara's first, and then Clair's. There was a third.

He opened his eyes. Where was he? What happened?

He lay there without moving, trying to get his bearings. He was on his back with his head facing away from the voices. He was in his bed, he determined, but why?

He thought back to what he remembered last. He was standing on the falls. He was fishing. He had slipped. Then the stranger was there. Had he seen the stranger or was he just dreaming again? There was a rhythmic pounding. What was that noise?

He focused on the third voice. Dana didn't know whose it was.

"He's lucky," the strange voice said. "He doesn't have any water in his lungs. When he hit his head it knocked him out cold. And then when he fell into the water his body instinctively made him hold his breath."

"It's a good thing you were there, Clair, or he would have surely drowned," the voice declared.

Clair was there? Dana thought. How'd he get there? Clair wasn't there. He was by himself. And then the stranger was there. This person has it wrong!

Dana turned to tell this person. He let out a loud moan. Now the pain hammered him with each heart beat, seemingly trying to split open his skull, nauseating him. So that's what the pounding was.

"He's awake," Barbara said softly.

Dana heard some rustling in the room. A bright light shone in his eyes, first one then the other. He tried to turn away but was unable to, as whoever was responsible had his hand on his forehead and was holding his eyelids open.

He let out a moan in protest but that was all he could do.

The light was gone.

"He'll be all right," the voice declared. "He's going to have one hell of a headache for a few days but he should be fine. Just let him rest. I'll give you some pills for him that should help the pain, but he'll be okay. It wouldn't be a bad idea to try and get him up and about later on tonight," the voice instructed. "Maybe you could try to get some supper into him."

"Thanks, Doc," Dana heard Clair say, "we'll do that. Let me walk you out."

Dana listened as the two made their way downstairs.

"It's just a good thing you were there, Clair, or who knows what we might be dealing with. Now how about you, Clair? Barbara says you have problems breathing..." Dana heard the doctor say, not hearing him finish, their voices fading as they made their way down the stairs.

Barbara spoke. "How are you feeling?"

Dana focused his eyes on her concerned face as she bent over him, putting her hand on his forehead.

"My head is pounding," Dana answered, grimacing as he spoke.

"Well, you rest," Barbara said. "Can I get you anything before I leave?"

"No," Dana responded. "Barbara?"

"Yes, Dana?" she answered.

"It wasn't Clair who was there, was it?" Dana said in short breaths, the intense pain making it hard to talk.

"Shhh," Barbara answered softly. "You get some rest and we'll talk later," she said reassuringly.

Dana felt a calmness envelope him as he closed his eyes. He could feel Barbara's presence, watching over him. Right now he just wanted to sleep.

CHAPTER 25

Dana could feel someone shaking him gently.

"Dana," whispered the voice. "Dana," came the whisper again, along with a gentle nudge.

He opened his eyes. He winced before he felt the pain that he knew from earlier would follow the *"thump, thump, thump."* It was as bad as earlier. It made him nauseous again.

"Dana," Barbara said, "you need to get up and try to eat something. I'll help you." Dana looked around the room. The bedroom light was on. He could tell from the darkness of the window it was nighttime.

"Come on," Barbara coaxed gently.

Dana lifted the sheets to swing his feet to the floor. Coolness rushed in, displacing the warmth. He shivered.

He was naked, he realized, as he tried to cover up.

Barbara caught the blankets and coaxed him again. "Come on," she said, "I'll help you. You need to get up." She reached down and tugged firmly on his hand. Dana's head hurt so much that having Barbara see him naked was the least of his worries.

Dana edged towards the side of the bed. His head pounded when he moved. He sat on the edge, shivering. Barbara had his underwear in her hands. She reached around his body and helped him stand.

"Here," she said. "I'll hold on to this side and you the other and then I can steady you as you put your leg through," she offered. Dana slipped one leg through the hole and then the other. Barbara, with her arm still around his waist, helped him pull them up. Dana sat back on the edge of the bed, dizziness overtaking him. His head throbbed. He put his hands on his head and felt the bandage he hadn't realized that was there. He traced it with his fingertips around to the back of his head, wincing as he felt the large, very tender knot that was there.

"Here," Barbara said, as she held out his pants.

Barbara helped Dana stand. They worked together as they had a moment ago, slipping on his pants. She sat him on the bed. Barbara squatted down and rolled on one of Dana's socks.

"You are a pretty lucky boy," Barbara said, working on the second sock. "The doctor said you'll be fine in a couple days."

Dana listened to her, not knowing or really wanting to respond. He was groggy, sick to his stomach and he was quite sure his head was going to burst. Barbara helped him put his shirt on. Dana was glad it had buttons and didn't have to be slipped over his head.

"Ready?" Barbara asked, helping him stand.

"What time is it?" Dana asked as they made their way to the door.

"A few minutes after eight," Barbara responded. "Clair will be in in a few minutes."

"Chores," Dana said apologetically.

"You don't need to be worrying about that," Barbara scolded. "Besides, you're in no condition for chores at this moment. You're going to take a couple days off."

"But, Clair," Dana started.

"You don't need to worry about Clair," Barbara said, cutting Dana off in mid-sentence. "He'll be just fine."

When it hurt just to talk, never mind walking, as the two navigated down the stairs, Dana knew it was no time to argue. Besides, on a good day he was no match for Barbara, especially when she was determined as she was now.

Barbara guided Dana to the kitchen table and sat him down. She had been baking. Dana could smell it. The heat from the stove felt good as Dana shivered again.

"Here," she said, holding out a couple tablets in one hand and a glass of water in the other. "The Doctor said these would help your headache." Dana put the pills in his mouth and chased them with the water. He took several sips. *Horse pills,* he thought, referring to their size.

Dana heard the familiar sound of Clair coming through the outside door into the wood shed. His mind visually followed him as he made his way to the kitchen mud room door.

"Come on, boy," he heard Clair say, and thought for an instant he was talking to him.

Around the corner came Duke. That was unusual for two reasons. Duke had never been in the house since Dana had lived there, and secondly, he was usually not around at this time of night, preferring to be wherever it was he stayed.

Duke made a beeline to Dana, tail wagging a hundred miles an hour, tongue hanging out as if he was smiling at him.

"He just wanted to make sure you were okay," Clair said from around the corner.

Dana slid his chair around to greet his little buddy. Holding one hand under Duke's chin, Dana stroked his nose, sliding his hand to the top of his head, and then stopping to scratch his ears. He did it several times as Duke tried to repeatedly lick him.

"I'm okay," Dana said aloud to the dog, repeating the petting motion several more times, each time repeating he was okay. Duke seemed satisfied as he looked around, checking out the surroundings, and then went to the door asking to be let out.

Barbara went to let him out the mud room door. She had something in her hand, which Dana guessed was a donut. He heard her talk to the dog. "Here you go, now you have a good night."

Clair had finished taking off his boots and made his way into the kitchen.

"You gonna make it?" he asked Dana.

"I'll be fine," Dana replied, embarrassed about his lack in judgment. Of all people, Clair was who he didn't want to disappoint. Clair had specifically asked him not to go on the other side of the river. Technically, he hadn't, but it was splitting hairs to argue that point. He had a trust with Clair. To have Clair question that trust, to have him ever have to wonder if Dana would do as he was asked was unthinkable to him.

"I'm sorry," he blurted out, fighting back tears, surprised that it came out that way, not realizing it until he said it, that as much as he was embarrassed, he was sorry. Clair stepped over to the table, putting his big calloused hand on the back of Dana's neck, gently squeezing.

"I know you are, son," he said as he caressed the back of his neck pulling him closer to him, "I'm just glad you're okay."

Clair turned to walk into the bathroom to wash up. Dana used the back of his hand to wipe his eyes. Barbara, who had been standing at the stove preparing supper, walked over and handed Dana a handkerchief. "Here," she said when Dana didn't see her.

He used it to dry his eyes, and then blew his nose. "Ow," he said, as blowing his nose hurt his pounding head. The three ate supper in silence, except for Barbara's prodding of Dana to eat.

Dana wasn't hungry. He thought about Barbara's assurance earlier that they would talk later. He wasn't even interested it that. He wanted to go to bed. He excused himself when he finished his plate. He washed up in the bathroom and brushed his teeth, pausing to look at himself and his bandaged head in the mirror.

At least Clair isn't mad, he thought, as he studied the bandage, turning to look as far back of his head as the mirror allowed. *I don't think he is very proud, but at least he's not mad.*

Clair and Barbara were still at the table when he came out of the bathroom.

"I'll be ready for chores in the morning," he announced to both of them.

"Think again," Barbara said immediately. "I told you earlier you had a couple days off and it is not up for discussion." Barbara had put her foot down. It would have been a foolish person who crossed that line. Maybe Clair could, but only when it came to himself. Right now he didn't have a dog in the fight.

"Barbara's right," Clair said, backing up his wife's decision. "We do have some things that we would like to discuss with you tomorrow though. So sleep in, get better, and enjoy your time off," Clair said, putting an end to any more talk of tomorrow's chores.

Dana had been thoroughly trumped. Besides, he really didn't feel that good anyways.

He made his way upstairs and was asleep before his head hit the pillow.

Chapter 26

Dana slept well. He was woken sometime in the night by Barbara, who had some more pills for him to take, but was asleep again before he looked at the clock.

He awoke the next morning and was surprised that it was 8:30.

He cautiously moved his head, expecting to feel the pain that he had felt the night before. It still hurt but the thumping was gone. He gingerly swung his feet out of bed, realizing that he had slept in his clothes. Dana sat on the edge before he stood up. Today, he was sure, he would find out who the stranger was. Maybe he could finally meet him face to face and thank him. Thank him for saving him from drowning, and also for the food that he had delivered to the people of Mill village.

That would be neat.

Dana stood up, again thankful that the pounding in his head had stopped. He made his way downstairs. Clair had just walked in.

"Give him a little time off and he sleeps til noon," Clair teased.

"I know," Dana said.

"How do you feel this morning?" Barbara asked, as she met him with his two pills and a glass of water.

"A lot better," he replied as he washed his pills down.

"I'm glad," she said, and added "you look more like yourself, except for your turban," she said, picking on his bandage.

Dana laughed, the image from the mirror the night before popping into his head.

"We'll take a peek after breakfast to see what it looks like," Barbara said. "If it has stopped seeping it'll probably be okay to go without."

"Sounds good to me," Dana replied.

Barbara had breakfast ready. All the scrambled eggs, ham steak, home fries and homemade toast that they wanted to eat. Dana was hungry. He hadn't eaten much yesterday and breakfast tasted good. Dana helped Barbara clear the table. "Just stack them in the sink and I'll do them after. Come sit at the table," Barbara said. "Clair and I want to talk with you."

Dana, in the last thirty hours, had seen seriousness from Barbara that he had never witnessed. He sensed a strength that could only come from the grit and determination of carving out a living in the beautiful but harsh northern Vermont climate working side by side with her husband.

Dana had always thought Clair was the tough one, with Barbara casting a supporting role. He, in the short time span of one day plus a little more, learned that it truly took both of them to make it work. If both weren't as equally determined, this life would eat you up. Things could go sour in only a moment, as his near-drowning proved to him.

Leadership roles had changed. It was Barbara at this moment who was the leader and Clair was supporting her.

Dana took his usual spot at the table. Barbara took a deep breath and began to talk.

"I think you know that we consider you one of the family," she began, looking Dana square in the eyes. "We've known you for a long time. Longer than what you know. We were friends with your grandfather and grandmother. We didn't do a lot of things together but when you own land that abuts another person's you can't help but to have some interaction."

Dana nodded to acknowledge but said nothing, letting her continue.

"When your grandmother died of cancer we helped raise your mother some," Barbara continued. "She was only twelve and it was very hard on her to watch her mother suffer the way she did. It was hard on both your grandfather and mother. They missed her so much."

Barbara paused to take a drink of water and continued.

"Your grandfather was a very private man of few words and it was hard on him, as you can imagine, losing a wife, raising a young daughter, especially when he and your mother didn't communicate well. They didn't know how. Your grandmother was their glue."

Dana nodded again, listening intently.

"There were feelings that they both had but were unable to tell one another, and although they loved each other very much, they drifted apart. Your grandfather spent most of his time in the barn or in the hay fields or in the woods," Barbara explained, "and your mother was left to fend for herself when he wasn't here. Probably even when he was," she added. "Your grandfather tried in his way to make it right. He even hired a man who was married, to help on the farm, and moved both the hired man and his wife into the house to help raise your mother. Your mother resented another woman in the house, especially one trying to act as her mother, and it just caused more problems between your mother and grandfather."

Dana was learning in a few minutes about his family what he had waited a lifetime for. He wasn't about to interrupt. Clair all the while was sitting quietly, watching them both, fidgeting with his hands.

Barbara continued on. "And then your mother met your father in school. We didn't know him. We can't tell you much about him, other than your grandfather and he hated one another. But your mother loved him. She told me that he understood her and I really didn't know what she meant by that, but I could only guess that he paid attention to her. Certainly something she was starved for. Before long they eloped, because you were on the way, and your mother wanted to be married before you were born." Barbara smiled for the first time since starting the story, but her pause was brief before she continued again.

"That was just too much for your grandfather. He disowned her. They didn't speak until after you were born. She brought you there when you were just a month old, and he was proud." Barbara was now beaming, looking past Dana as if she was watching Dana's grandfather hold him.

Dana waited for Barbara to continue.

"They started to talk again, and just before you were a year old your parents and you moved into the farm house with your grandfather. It didn't last long. Your father and he just couldn't get along." Barbara stopped for a moment and looked at Clair. She reached her hand out for his as if she needed his strength to continue. He put his hand on top of hers. Barbara looked at Dana and started again.

"The day that it happened," she said, pausing to look at Dana to see if he knew what day she was talking about. She started again.

"The day your parents were killed they stopped here as they were leaving to say goodbye. You were standing in the back seat, not a care in the world, just happy to be going for a ride. Both Clair and I held you to say goodbye but you just wanted to ride. We gave you back to your mother, wished both of them well, waved goodbye to you and, well..." Barbara stopped speaking. She clinched Clair's hand tighter and her voice got soft as she looked down at the table and then back to Dana and continue, "Well, then hours later we heard what happened. We couldn't believe it. We were devastated." Barbara paused to dab the corners of her eyes with a cloth. She was trying hard to keep herself from getting too emotional to continue.

Dana felt almost like he wasn't there. Almost as if he was watching a picture show instead. It was just so much information. Information that he had felt was long lost and had given up on ever knowing. This was his life being told by people who were there. People who knew his family and now considered him part of theirs. He was anxious to hear more.

Clair cleared his throat and looked down and then to Barbara. Barbara dabbed the corners of her eyes again.

Clair cleared his throat again and began to speak.

"We could see the black smoke first," Clair said, motioning with his chin towards Dana's land. "Before I could get there I could see the flames."

"I pulled up the drive and was the first one there. Both the house and barn were totally gone. I didn't know which way to go. I watched, helplessly, there was nothing I could do but wait for the others," Clair said. He sounded apologetic.

Clair began again, "I was standing there when the Sheriff came tearing in. He called me Joe at first until I told him Joe was nowhere to be found. There wasn't a chance to save anything, but I imagine that's how Joe wanted it. We have never judged him. A man sometimes does, right or wrong, what he thinks he has to do."

They were both silent as they looked at one another.

Dana felt selfish at that moment. He was hearing about the death of his family, watching through their eyes, hearing Barbara and Clair painfully tell what they had witnessed or knew to be true. He felt bad for them and if they didn't want to say anymore, he understood. He had learned so much in a half hour. He was ready to tell them it was okay, to console them.

But they had more to tell.

Barbara spoke this time. “We heard about the miracle baby and couldn’t believe it. Yes Dana, that’s what they called you; the miracle baby.” Dana must have showed surprise and Barbara picked up on it. *It’s all a surprise to me,* he thought, at least in this much detail.

She continued again. “We waited for a couple hours on the porch because we heard you were coming home, coming back to Ethenburg. We could hear the sirens for at least five miles and then we could see all the flashing lights. We waited until everyone passed and we followed. We came into town as everyone was making their way into the Town Hall. We followed and took a seat in the back.”

“You were there?” Dana asked, surprised.

“Yes,” Clair and Barbara answered at the same time.

“We were there to bring you home with us, but so were a lot of other people,” Barbara said.

Dana was blown away. He had heard through bits and pieces over the years about that night, the events of that day, but this was almost as if he was there now.

“Please”, Dana said, “if you can go on I’d like to hear the rest.”

“Well,” Barbara started, “when they started the discussion about where you would go it was quite heated. Clair was just about to speak up when your Aunt Polly and Uncle David came in. We thought right then and there it was settled, family should always go to family, although a lot of people who were sticking their noses in where it didn’t belong, didn’t agree. We were so happy that it turned out that way.”

Dana was happy. To be told about his life, to know his history, his lineage, was what he had always wanted to know. That was what anyone would want to know. Where did I come from? Who am I? The discouraging part for Dana was that he had come from the town he now lived in, had always lived in, and nobody was ever able to tell him about his life, how he came to be. Clair and Barbara had now made him whole.

"Of course you know about Robert Marcoux," Clair started. "One of the bank board members had called me and told me what he was up to. I called the lawyer, Fred Summers, to tell him what I was up to and asked him what time the paperwork was to be signed. I asked Fred to make sure that Robert was there before I came in. I wanted him to feel something that he didn't want to for all the bad things he has done to others. Fred played it perfectly. He even got Marcoux to pay him for all his legal fees. It was beautiful," Clair said, smiling ear to ear. "Joe Lanou never intended for Robert Marcoux to own his land. That I'm sure of," Clair stated.

"So that's it?" Dana asked. "That's what you wanted to tell me?" he said softly.

"No," Barbara said, "we have one last piece of the puzzle. Something that you have known about but haven't dared to ask, and something that we weren't prepared to tell."

How could I have forgotten? he wondered. He really felt so selfish this time that he apologized.

"No need to," Clair said, as he began to speak.

"I have a friend who has helped me for years and thank God that he has because yesterday would have turned out a whole lot different. Instead of talking to you today we could have been planning your funeral. I can't tell you what that would have done to me or Barbara."

Clair stopped and looked at Barbara as they reached for each other's hand again.

"Our friend's name is Stanley and he lives on his brother's land in a shack no bigger than the size of this table," Clair said motioning at the long kitchen table that they ate at every day but only used a small corner of.

"No kidding!" Clair said as he looked at Dana, measuring the table.

"Stanley," Clair said, "has a drinking problem, but when he isn't drinking he's a hell of a nice guy and a hard worker. For whatever reason, I've never asked him, but Stanley and his brother do not get along, even though his brother helps him out and would not let anything bad happen to him. Anyways, Stanley has a lot of pride. Sometimes a man's pride can get in the way of reason, but Stanley doesn't want his brother to know that he works. So we don't tell anyone. Do you understand, Dana?" Clair asked.

"Stanley's the one who saved me yesterday?" Dana asked.

"Yes," Clair said.

"And Stanley's the person who helps you in the woods?" Dana asked again.

"Stanley has helped me in a lot of places, but yes, he has helped me this year in the woods," Clair fessed up.

"Then Stanley is the same guy who I saw and heard one night in the kitchen a couple months ago, and also saw late one night leaving food at my neighbor's and at Polly's in Mill village!" Dana exclaimed.

"Yes," Barbara smiled. "That's our Stanley."

"We were happy that Polly and David could take you home to raise you but we knew they didn't have a lot of money. We wanted to help," Barbara said.

"Stanley's up all hours of the night and walks for miles, so we asked him to leave some food on your doorstep. At first he left it at the wrong house, but we didn't want to stop leaving food there, and then we decided we might as well leave it in a couple of places that had kids. They could certainly use it," Barbara explained proudly.

"Just so I'm clear," Dana asked, "Stanley wears the funny hat?"

"That's his disguise," Clair laughed.

"Oh it's a good one," Dana said, laughing, "it had me fooled! Can I ask one last question?"

"Sure," Clair said, "go ahead."

"Can I meet Stanley some day to thank him?"

Barbara looked at Clair and answered, "Some day ,yes, when Stanley says it's okay."

"Fair enough?" Clair asked, adding "our secret about Stanley is safe with you?"

"Yes," Dana said, "I won't tell anyone, I promise. I'm just happy to know that you weren't dragging all that wood yourself!" Dana laughed.

Clair and Barbara burst out laughing.

"Dana," Barbara said, "I have something else for you."

"What's that?" Dana said.

"I'll be right back," she said, as she slid her chair away from the table and disappeared to her bedroom. She returned with a small wooden box with some faded colorful painting on top with a small metal clasp.

"Here," she said handing it to him.

"What is this?" Dana asked curiously.

"Well," said Barbara, "seeing how you're not going to the barn tonight you need something to do. In this box are pictures of all of your family."

"All of them?" he asked quietly.

"Yes," she answered, "all that we know about."

Dana sat silently. He had never seen a picture of anyone. Not his grandfather, his mother, his father, grandmother, none of them. Dana stood up with the box and stood between Clair and Barbara, he reached out to them. He began to cry as the three of them hugged in the kitchen.

Chapter 27

Dana recovered from his near drowning. His headaches lasted for a few days but Barbara only made him miss chores four times. Dana pored through the pictures that Barbara had given him.

Most of his mother's school pictures were in the box, but only one of his father's. Dana guessed it was one that his father had given to his mother. There were four of his grandfather. Two with his family, one with his wife, Dana's grandmother, and the other of him by himself, standing next to a team of horses hauling a load of loose hay.

There were scattered other pictures as well. Some of his grandmother and some Dana didn't recognize. He'd ask Barbara in time if she knew who they were, he decided.

There was an article from the paper complete with a picture of the mangled car that had taken Dana's parents life. He didn't read the article. *Not now, but sometime,* he told himself. The bold headlines read, "Miracle baby survives fatal crash!" Just like Barbara had said. Dana was happy to have the pictures. He was surprised that he didn't feel a bigger connection to them, but their faces weren't familiar to him.

Dana held up the pictures of his parents one by one and compared them to his own image in the mirror. He could see some similarities, but nothing concrete. He had been told a few times by strangers he had been introduced to that he looked like his grandfather. He couldn't tell by the comparisons that he conducted. Maybe they had the same build or posture. Dana couldn't be sure.

Dana took his grandfather's picture to his bedroom window and held it towards his land. He could just make out the rise of where the house and barn had been. Dana tried to envision his grandfather in that spot with the team of horses and the load of hay as he held up the picture. It was just a picture.

Dana moved the picture that he held straight out in his arm towards Granite Hill. Dana smiled, he could see him there now, his grandfather, standing beside his wood processor.

Chapter 28

School had started for the new year. Dana now was officially part of the Ethenburg High School freshman Class of 1954.

It was funny to see some of his classmates that he hadn't seen since May and how much their appearance had changed. Others had commented about him but he didn't feel any different. The only difference was that he now was on the third floor with all of the high school kids. There were thirty-six kids total that Dana had counted. Give or take one or two.

Clair still gave him a ride to school and picked him up. Dana did chores morning and night. Some of the kids played sports but Dana wasn't interested. He preferred to come home to the farm.

Around the farm, Clair and Dana were getting ready for winter. It was late September and it would come quick enough. If you didn't get done what was needed then it would probably have to wait until spring. The pace certainly slowed some in the fall.

The hay crops were in, all of the piles of Dana's wood were sold and gone with only a little bit of money left to be collected. The farm house cellar was filled with big chunks of wood for the house furnace and the smaller pieces of fine split wood for the kitchen cook stove were piled in the wood shed they used as their entrance.

The surrounding mountainsides were on fire with brilliant fall colors of bright oranges, crisp yellows, and flaming reds. Not just the mountainsides, every tree that had leaves, but that's where it was most pronounced.

They had butchered a beef which was stored in the freezer and when deer season came in November, between the both of them, maybe they would be able to put a deer or two in the freezer.

The Phillips farm was ready for winter.

In between chores, if Clair wanted to, he could take it easier. Clair had mentioned he wanted to service the wood processor. He told Dana that the engine oil and filter should be changed on the compressor and that a new filter for the hydraulic oil should be installed. The two batteries should be disconnected and brought home, too.

It was just a couple-hour job at best that Clair could do when Dana was in school. Clair's knee was bothering him quite a bit and he, in the last month, had times when he was really short of breath, which he attributed to the new hay in the barn. Barbara was concerned and Dana had heard more than once about "the stubborn old fool."

Dana worked it so that he could get to the barn ahead of Clair. When he woke in the morning he went straight to the barn. The extra fifteen minutes let him get ahead of Clair and besides, he never did develop a taste for coffee.

Clair would be all right, Dana was sure. He was tough. His knee was troublesome and his breathing was probably because he was coming down with a cold.

It was Friday, the first week of November as Clair gave Dana a ride to school.

"I'm going to service the wood processor today," Clair announced to Dana.

"Today?" Dana said. "If you wait until tomorrow I'll help," Dana suggested.

"Suppose to rain tomorrow and I'd just as soon do it today," Clair said. "Besides, I think our friend Stanley needs a little booze money. If I can get him to drive the tractor over," Clair continued, "I'd bring my truck and pick up the rest of the limb wood for the kitchen stove. We don't really need it but it doesn't do it any good to sit out there all winter," he justified.

Dana agreed. He knew that's what was going to happen and left it at that.

"Speaking of money," Clair spoke again, "The Davis' dropped off the last bit of money they owed you for the wood. I think if I'm not mistaken, that cleans you up."

"That's great," Dana answered, "why don't you use some of that to pay Stanley today?"

"Stanley's fine," Clair replied. "We'll take care of that."

The truck was approaching the common. All the maples that surrounded the green had turned their brilliant colors as well.

"What a picturesque little village we have here," Clair remarked as he drove by the common, taking a right at the far end and pointing the truck towards the school.

"You did a great job this summer with the wood, Dana," Clair said. "Not just the wood, but with everything else as well," Clair added. Dana processed Clair's comment. He needed to respond but it had caught him off guard.

The school was in sight and Clair was slowing to make the left-hand turn. Before Dana could respond, Clair spoke again, looking straight ahead. "I know I've never said this, but I'm proud of you, Dana."

Dana fought back his emotion, biting his lower lip. He looked at Clair, who was still staring ahead, waiting for a school bus to turn.

Dana, trying to think of the words that wouldn't come, just spoke. "I want to thank you Clair, you and Barbara. I want to thank you both for the person that I've become. It is because of you two. You say that you're proud of me, Clair? I'm proud of you. I could only wish to be half the man you are." Dana looked at Clair. He had turned towards the driver side window. The truck had stopped just before the school.

Dana grabbed his books and opened the door to get out.

"See you this afternoon," he said to Clair, "and don't be late," Dana chided.

Clair kept looking towards the glass and waved his hand towards Dana as if to say, 'just get going.' Dana walked up the stairs to the front double doors turning to watch the old Ford leave.

Half the man? Dana thought. *Even those would be big shoes to fill.*

Dana ran inside to join his classmates.

Before Dana knew it, it was lunch time. The school didn't have a cafeteria, so the high school kids helped the teachers shepherd the younger kids up the hill towards town to the Town Hall where there was a kitchen. Here lunch was served. When lunch was over, the procession headed back to the school to continue their studies. The ritual was done every day that there was school, no matter what the weather was like.

It was a few minutes past one. Dana had just returned from lunch.

Dana had just opened his History book when he heard some commotion in the hallway. A disturbance like maybe a fistfight or something, but without the loudness. This wasn't loud, but it wasn't right either.

Mr. Wright, the principal entered the class room. Behind him, stopping at the doorway was the Sheriff. Mr. Wright made his way to the front of the class and whispered in the ear of Ms. Jackman, the History teacher.

Dana watched, not feeling right as Ms. Jackman's eyes got large and she looked at Dana.

Dana felt the pit of his stomach turn and instantly started to sweat. He sat in his seat as the two approached and prayed that they would pass by him. But they didn't.

"Dana," Ms. Jackman spoke. "You need to go with Mr. Wright and the officer."

The classroom was completely silent as Dana began to gather his books.

"Don't worry about those," the teacher spoke, "we'll get them to you."

Dana got to his feet, his knees felt feeble as he followed the Principal to the door, and said hello softly to the Sheriff.

The Sheriff nodded and followed them out the door.

They walked in single file down the three flights of stairs. Dana held the railing for support. His mind raced. Was it David or Polly or Barbara or Clair? He knew it was at least one of them.

Mr. Wright stopped at the front door and turned to the other two as they reached the last stair.

"Dana," Mr. Wright continued, "something bad has happened and you need to go with Officer Briar. He will tell you what he can."

Dana could hardly form the words, his mouth was so dry and he was scared.

"Thank you," he said to Mr. Wright.

"Right this way, Sir," Officer Briar said to Dana as he held the door for him.

"Thank you," Dana said again as he exited the school.

"Why don't you sit in the front," the officer offered.

The officer sat behind the wheel, started the car and spun some in the dirt as he left the school. He flicked on his siren when he was at the main road. Dana guessed that the lights were probably on too.

When they reached the common the Sheriff's car turned left towards the farm.

Dana turned to the Sheriff and asked him, "Is it Barbara or Clair?"

"Clair, Sir," the officer answered.

The Sheriff was driving at a great speed. Dana was praying under his breath that it was just an accident. He didn't dare or want to ask the officer anything else.

The officer spoke to Dana, "It was probably fifteen or sixteen years ago I met you for the first time," he said. "I'm glad you're doing okay. If you need anything, my name is Officer Briar."

"Thank you," Dana said. "Thank you."

The Sheriff pulled into the yard and shut his siren off. There were a lot of strange vehicles in the yard, none that Dana recognized.

Dana ran through the wood shed and burst into the kitchen. He could see a couple people standing between the sitting room and kitchen, facing the sitting room. They turned to acknowledge Dana.

Dana brushed by them into the sitting room, looking for Clair. Barbara was sitting on the couch, with her friend Alice on one side of her and Aunt Polly on the other. They were crying. Dana rushed over and knelt down in front of Barbara. She reached for him and wrapped her arms around him, sobbing.

Dana was scared as he hugged her. He whispered in her ear. "Where is he? Where's Clair?"

Barbara pulled away and wiped her tears, looking Dana in his eyes. "He's gone Dana, he's gone," she said softly, reaching for him again, sobbing uncontrollably, burying her head in his shoulders.

Polly reached over and hugged the two. The three embraced.

Dana tried to cry. The tears wouldn't come. He was so scared. *What will we do?* he thought. *I've got to take care of Barbara but without Clair what will we do?* His mind raced, searching for an answer.

The three held on for a moment longer.

Barbara was the first to pull away. She and Dana held each other at arm's length. They looked at one another. Dana could see her change before him.

Barbara reached to Dana with her hand and caressed his cheek. Dana watched as she composed herself. As if she was reading his mind she whispered to Dana, "We'll be okay, we might miss him every day, but we'll be okay." Dana could feel the strength flowing into his body as they held one another.

He wasn't scared anymore.

Barbara whispered again, "We have company that needs attending to, and Polly has offered to help," as Barbara reached over and pulled Polly towards them, forming a triangle. The three took a moment longer in their huddle as if to draw strength. Barbara cleared her throat, signaling that they had work to do. They released their grips. Barbara stood and walked towards the others who had formed behind them and greeted them.

Dana and Polly stood and faced one another. He looked over at David, who was standing off to the side, and motioned him over. David walked the couple steps to them. Dana wrapped his arms around them.

"I love you guys," Dana said, "I've always known you were there for me."

The crowds of people continued to come. Dana and Barbara, with the help of Polly and David, greeted them and attended to their needs.

Hot dishes arrived and needed to be stored. Some were put on the table and served to the people who came to offer their condolences.

The Rabideau brothers showed up and would not take no for an answer. They would do chores for a couple of days anyways, and then they would determine if they were needed more. Robert made it plain and simple. It was not Dana's decision, it was his.

"Clair was a good man and dis is da very lease we could do." He added, "If Bernard and Gaston don' do a good job, you let me know." Dana thanked him and assured him that he had faith in his brothers.

It was close to five, and the crowd had thinned. Barbara caught Dana's eye and motioned him over. Dana walked over and bent over so Barbara could whisper to him.

"There is a tractor that is left in the woods from today. I know Clair would not want it left there overnight," she said.

Dana nodded in agreement. "I'll run over and get it now before it gets dark," he assured her. "Let Polly and David know that I'll give them a ride home when I get back if they're ready," Dana said.

"I will," Barbara said.

Dana snuck out through the back kitchen door so that the people still there wouldn't see him leave, thinking they had to leave as well. Dana walked to the drive and started to jog the couple miles. It wouldn't take him long.

He thought back to this morning, as he picked a pace that was comfortable to maintain, to Clair's and his goodbye. He wondered if he had known, maybe somehow or some way. It was only a moment, it seemed, and he had turned and run through the open gate of their property line.

You know something, he thought to himself, *Clair had always said to close the gates behind you. The only times that they hadn't, something bad had happened. From now on, the gates will always be closed.*

Dana jogged towards the maples. They were beautiful in all their colors. *I guess there could be a lot worse places to draw your last breath,* Dana decided.

The clearing was coming. Without the noise of a tractor, the waterfall sounded more ominous.

Dana hadn't given it a thought. He hadn't been back since he had almost drowned. He broke out into the clearing, stopping to gaze upwards at the face of the granite cliffs. He admired, as he seemed to do every time he came, the ruggedness, the bare beauty of the granite wall. Dana heard the words come from his mouth asking God to give him strength and to watch over them.

Dana followed from the top, the jagged lines the rock formed working his gaze to the bottom.

"Whoa!" he said out loud, there was Duke standing in the middle of the falls. Right where Dana had fallen. It had startled him.

"Come on, boy," Dana called. "Come on."

Duke stayed still, watching Dana.

"Duke," Dana said sternly, "Come!" as he slapped his knee.

Duke turned and faced away from Dana.

What's wrong with him? Dana wondered. *He always comes when I call him.*

Dana walked to the edge of the river. "Duke!" he yelled louder, thinking that maybe he hadn't heard him over the sound of the river.

Duke walked to the far side and turned to look at Dana.

"I'm not fooling Duke, let's go," Dana pleaded.

Duke took another step towards the ledges.

"I'm not coming over there to get you," Dana said to the dog. "Come here!" he commanded.

Duke looked at Dana and took another step and faced Dana so that only his head and shoulders could be seen. Dana looked at the river racing by. *Why won't he come?* Dana wondered. *He has to be hurt someway,* Dana reasoned, *otherwise he would come as he always does when I call.*

Dana stood on the edge of the river. The water thundered over the falls where a couple months before he almost lost his life.

Clair's voice echoed in his head, "Promise me, Dana, you will never go on that side of the river. Am I clear, Dana?"

"Yes Clair, you are," he said out loud, "But Duke is in trouble."

Dana took a step into the water. The current seemed fierce as he stepped back onto the shore.

"Duke, get your ass over here right now!" Dana hollered through clenched teeth. "I mean it!"

Duke turned and disappeared.

"Son of a bitch, Jesus Christ," Dana swore, almost out of his mind.

With the words of Clair ringing in his head, he stepped into the water, on to the rock pathway. He focused on the other side of the river and walked briskly across, looking only forward, not down at his feet or at the water crashing over the edge to his right.

He reached the other side and almost collapsed. He had held his breath the whole way across.

"Duke!" he yelled, peering up at the rock trail that was hidden from view from the east side of the river. "Where are you?"

Duke showed himself further up for a brief moment, but disappeared again.

"You had better be injured, dog," Dana threatened, "because if you're not you're going to be."

Dana made his way up the trail, walking cautiously, looking for booby traps, as Clair had called them. He advanced up about a hundred feet where the trail turned away from the river.

Dana's heart was pounding. He didn't dare to call for the dog. His senses were on high alert.

This is too much, he thought. *I'm going to turn back, I have to,* he told himself. His concern for Duke and curiosity drove him just a little further. The trail narrowed and then it looked as if it came to a dead end twenty feet or so away. Dana stopped and studied it. Had he taken a wrong turn?

He couldn't have, there was only one trail. He walked to what appeared to be the face of the cliff.

His mind raced. *It's a door! What's a door doing here? A friggin' door, right here?* His mind searched for any reasonable answer.

Dana studied it. It blended with the granite face until you were right on top of it.

He studied it closer. *It's ajar some. That's why I can see it.*

His mind was whirling a hundred miles an hour. Dana reached for the door and pushed it forward. It swung easily until it showed a dimly lit room.

This just doesn't make sense, this just isn't right. Maybe the smugglers are still here, but this isn't right, his mind raced.

Dana stepped into the room. It was warm, and the soft glow from a kerosene lantern with the wick turned low hanging from the ceiling across the room only lit up part of the room. Dana shut the door behind him. Strangely, it felt like he belonged here.

He let his eyes get accustomed to the darkness, but the room was deep and it was still dark in places. There was a table in the center. Dana took a couple cautious steps towards it, stopping to let his eyes adjust. He could hear something. It was breathing, panting.

Oh God, he thought, *I hope that's Duke.*

"Duke," he said softly. He heard the panting come towards him. Duke began to take shape out of the shadows. He reached to pet him as Duke licked his hand, never taking his eyes from the further parts of the room.

He could sense another. "I'm Dana," he announced.

There was a pause. Dana could hear something come towards the light. He could start to make out an outline of someone. The figure stopped.

"I know," it answered back softly.

"Who are you?" Dana asked. "Do I know you?"

"You do," the figure said.

"Please," Dana said, "Come closer so I can see you."

Dana could hear the rustling of movement. The figure moved towards him some more. Dana could make out the distinctive hat, the three corner hat that he had known for so long.

"Please," Dana said, "I have only known you by your hat, but Clair and Barbara have told me who you are and I have a lot to thank you for."

The stranger spoke. "Sometimes we are not who you think we are. Sometimes there needs to be deception."

Dana listened to the voice speak; it was the man in the kitchen who he saw through the register, and also the one who called out his name when he was drowning. Dana swallowed hard, and spoke. "You are who I think you are," Dana said. "You are the person who I have known for a long time. I recognize your voice."

The man moved closer to the light. Dana could make out some of the features of his face. The man stepped into the light completely. Dana recognized him. Not the hat but him. He had seen him, or rather, he had seen his picture.

Dana spoke again. "You are Stanley, right?" he asked.

The man sighed. "No Dana, I'm sorry but my name isn't Stanley. I know that's what we told you but that's what we had to do."

"We," Dana asked, "as in Barbara and Clair?"

The man nodded his head yes.

"Then if you're not Stanley, then who are you?" Dana asked.

"My name is Joseph. Joseph Lanou. I'm your grandfather."

Made in the USA
San Bernardino, CA
03 August 2016